DUNE

LEXICON & LORE

Unofficial. Independent. Created with love.

EXPLORE OTHER GREAT UNIVERSES

Some fictional worlds stay with us forever. We read them. Reread them. Study them. Live in them.

This book is part of the "Great Universes" collection — a fan-created, unofficial series dedicated to exploring the most legendary fictional worlds, one universe at a time.

Each volume is written with care, curiosity, and love for the original.

Lore, themes, characters, symbols — from a reader's perspective.

Curious what else we've explored?

Search for "Great Universes" or "Peregrine Wilder" in your bookstore of choice — and continue the adventure.

Journey Through Fictional Worlds, One Universe at a Time

Copyright © 2025 by Peregrine Wilder

Copyright fuels creativity, supports diverse voices, and nurtures a culture of deep reading and discovery. Thank you for purchasing a legitimate edition of this book and for respecting copyright by not reproducing, scanning, or distributing any part of it in any form without permission.

By doing so, you support independent publishing and help authors create thoughtful, reader-focused content.

Disclaimer:

This is an unofficial, fan-created companion book. It is not licensed by, affiliated with, or endorsed by Herbert Properties LLC or any other rights holders.

Names, characters, terminology, and references from the Dune universe are used for educational, analytical, and transformative purposes only. All original material in this volume is the intellectual property of the author.

This book was created with admiration for the source material and with the intent to enrich the reading experience of fellow fans.

Legal Notice:

This companion book is intended for educational, analytical, and entertainment purposes only. The views expressed are solely those of the author. The reader assumes full responsibility for any use of the material herein.

Compliance with local, national, and international laws is the sole responsibility of the reader.

Neither the author nor the publisher assumes liability for any consequences resulting from the application or interpretation of the content.

Officially registered with ProtectMyWork.com. Protected under UK copyright law.

CONTENTS

✧ ◆ ✧

PART I: AN INTRODUCTION TO THE DUNE UNIVERSE 8

- ✦ Chapter 1. What is Dune? 9
- ✦ Chapter 2. The History of the Dune Saga 11
- ✦ Chapter 3. How to Read Dune? 14

PART II: THE WORLD AND ITS RULES 20

- ✦ Chapter 4: The Great Houses 21
- ✦ Chapter 5: The Desert Speaks — Key Terms 25
- ✦ Chapter 6: The Spice Must Flow 33
- ✦ Chapter 7: Hidden Schools and Open Powers 38
- ✦ Chapter 8: The Known Universe – Key Worlds 44
- ✦ Chapter 9: Machines and Men 50
- ✦ Chapter 10: The Fauna 56

PART III: CHARACTERS AND DEEP MEANING 62

- ✦ Chapter 11: House Atreides 64
- ✦ Chapter 12: The Loyal of House Atreides 70

- ✦ Chapter 13: The Fremen: Children of Dune........................... 75
- ✦ Chapter 14: House Harkonnen: The Path of Fear and Deceit 79
- ✦ Chapter 15: Radiance and Sunset of House Corrino................... 83
- ✦ Chapter 16: The Bene Gesserit.. 86
- ✦ Chapter 17: Other Key Figures of the Saga 90
- ✦ Chapter 18: Thematic and Philosophical Foundations of Dune.. 95

PART IV: THE DUNE PHENOMENON 104

- ✦ Chapter 19: Life Beyond the Book................................ 105
- ✦ Chapter 20: Dune as a Guide to Reality 109
- ✦ Chapter 21: 10 Grains of Sand That Shift the Inner Dunes....... 112

FINAL STEPS ON ARRAKIS.. 116

HOW TO USE THIS BOOK

In the silence after Dune, questions remain. This book listens—and answers. We begin at the outer edges:

Part I: The Sand Saga

First learning what Dune is, how it was created, and how best to approach it. From there, we step into the world itself:

Part II: The World and Its Rules

The Imperium's rules, the nature of Spice, key factions, worlds, and technologies.

Once the landscape is clear, we turn to the core of the saga: the people who shaped it—those whose choices built, broke, and remade empires—and the profound themes that pulse beneath the narrative.

Part III: Characters and Deep Meaning

> This section contains significant spoilers for the entire Frank Herbert saga, including character fates and major plot resolutions. New readers may wish to finish the hexalogy before proceeding here.

Part IV: Engaging with Dune: Legacy and Reflection

Exploring its legacy, and echoes in culture.

This final part also invites personal reflection through questions designed to open a dialogue between Herbert's vision and your own.

Let the ideas move you. Let the questions unfold.

Above all, let this journey become your own.

PART I. THE SAND SAGA: AN INTRODUCTION TO THE DUNE UNIVERSE

Where does Dune begin?

To understand its scale, you must start with the basics. This section offers the backstory of the saga, the structure of its universe, and the key entry points. It's your navigation chart through the sands—without it, it's easy to drown in the details.

Chapter 1. What is Dune?

« Deep in the human unconscious is a pervasive need for a logical universe that makes sense. But the real universe is always one step beyond logic. » — Leto II *(God Emperor of Dune, Thoughts/Records)*

Few works of science fiction have endured for over fifty years without losing their cultural and philosophical relevance. Frank Herbert's Dune is one of them. It is a novel that not only created its own mythology but became a cornerstone of the entire genre.

At its center lies a galactic empire with a thousand-year legacy. Artificial intelligence is forbidden; the functions of thinking machines are carried out by Mentats—humans trained to think with computational precision. The all-female order of the Bene Gesserit manipulates dynastic destinies behind the scenes, wielding genetics and social engineering as their tools. And on Arrakis—a barren, merciless desert planet—the spice melange is harvested: the substance that makes interstellar travel possible.

But the true essence of Dune isn't in its sands or its spice. Unlike most science fiction epics, it has no external enemy, no absolute evil. The central conflict is inward facing: a human being confronting the consequences of their own choices. This is a novel about the mutation of power, cultural memory, and religion as both instrument and trap. It's about the attempt to foresee the future—and the fear that it might actually come to pass.

Herbert builds a world where even prophecy is not liberation but a means of control. In this universe, ideas are more dangerous than weapons, and words are a strategic resource. It's a world in which one can easily become lost—so it's crucial to orient not by plot but by meaning.

> This book does not retell the novel; it's a guide through the structure of the world, its key themes and symbols, and the philosophy woven between the lines. If Dune is a myth, then this companion is your gear for the journey—for those who are ready to step into the story in earnest.

How to approach Dune (and should you at all)?

Reading Dune is not a test of speed—it's a test of attention. There is no flashy beginning where the hero receives a sword, a mentor, and an enemy. There is no obvious route. Herbert doesn't offer a tale; he offers an environment—dense, multilayered, and saturated with detail. To enter it, you must slow down. And—most unusually—you must trust the author, who does not explain but shows.

Herbert introduces terms without defining them. He names factions, worlds, and titles as if you already know them. This isn't negligence—it's deliberate. He doesn't want you to observe his universe from the outside. He wants you to step into it—as a newcomer in an alien culture, where you must observe, listen, adapt.

That's why so many readers feel lost at first—and that's precisely why a guide like this can help. Not as a cheat sheet, but as a map; not to explain the world but to help you find your place within it.

The difficulty of Dune is not in its language (which is surprisingly clear) but in its structure and its themes. There is no central conflict on the level of action. Instead, there are dozens of threads: politics, ecology, genetics, religion, history, memory. These don't align into a single vector—they form a web. And the more attentively you trace the patterns of that web, the more meaning you uncover. Or questions. More often than not—questions.

So, Dune is best read not quickly but in stages. With pauses. With rereading. It helps to return to the prologue after chapter five. It helps to read dialogue for the subtext, not the plot. It helps to abandon genre expectations and begin to treat the novel as a slow, subtle philosophical parable disguised as science fiction.

And no—it doesn't have to "click" right away. But if you enter with respect, without haste, and without looking for easy answers—it begins to speak. Not from the cover. Not from the blurb. But from within.

Before we dive into the structure of this universe, let's look back—and understand where this saga began.

Where did Arrakis come from? Why did Herbert choose this form?

And how did a novel rejected by over twenty publishers become one of the most influential books of the 20th century?

Chapter 2. The History of the Dune Saga

> *« Beginnings are such delicate times »* — Princess Irulan, from her historical writings, Dune

Origins

Dune didn't begin as a flash of inspiration—it began with a journalist's assignment. In the early 1960s, Frank Herbert was investigating the problem of dune stabilization along the Oregon coast. What started as research gradually grew, taking on unexpected questions and parallels—about humanity's interaction with nature, the consequences of intervention, and modes of survival. At some point, it ceased to be an article. It became a world.

Herbert wasn't a typical science fiction author. He had little interest in lasers, robots, or aliens. He was drawn to power, language, religion, psychology, ecology—and how they all form systems. Dune didn't grow out of fantasy but out of observations, concerns, and difficult questions. It was an experiment: what happens if we build a civilization where artificial intelligence is banned, but humans are enhanced? Where religion shapes politics, and environment shapes thought?

The Long Road to the Stars: Publication and Recognition

Writing the book took nearly six years. Publisher after publisher rejected it: too complex, too long, "too philosophical." Eventually, the novel was published by Chilton Books—a company best known for technical manuals for auto mechanics. The irony is striking and apt: a novel that dissects myth into component parts ended up in the hands of those who understand how to assemble intricate mechanisms.

Awards followed swiftly: the Hugo, the Nebula. But more importantly, a cultural life began. The book was reprinted, studied, adapted—and became a subject of academic interest, a rarity for science fiction.

The Dune Chronicles: Frank Herbert's Six-Book Cycle

The success of the original novel allowed Herbert to continue the story of Arrakis. Between 1969 and 1985, he wrote five direct sequels, expanding both the universe and its timeline. These novels, together with the original, from the classic cycle known as The Dune Chronicles. Each installment deepens the saga's core themes—power, prophecy, ecological transformation—and reveals a vision of humanity's distant future:

1. *Dune (1965)*: The birth of a legend. Introduces the desert world of Arrakis, the conflict of Great Houses, and the rise of young Paul Atreides, destined to confront his fate. Explores themes of ecology, politics, and the hidden potential of the human mind.

2. *Messiah (1969)*: The shadow of the myth. Examines the dark side of power and prophecy, portraying the tragic cost of Paul Muad'Dib's ascendancy.

3. *Children of Dune (1976)*: Legacy and transformation. Focuses on Paul's children and their struggle to shape the future of human-

ity amid Arrakis's ongoing metamorphosis.

4. *God Emperor of Dune (1981)*: The Age of the Titan. A bold leap 3,500 years into the Imperium's future. The galaxy has changed beyond recognition under the rule of a mysterious, near-mythical figure tied to Arrakis's distant past. This ruler steers humanity down an unfathomable Golden Path, posing profound questions about power, survival, and the essence of humanity.

5. *Heretics of Dune (1984)*: A new era, new threats. Fifteen hundred years after the God Emperor's death, the Imperium and humanity have dispersed into uncharted regions of space. The ancient Bene Gesserit sisterhood now struggles to preserve its influence as returning forces from the Scattering bring unexpected orders and dangers.

6. *Chapterhouse Dune (1985)*: The master's finale. In the gripping conclusion of Herbert's saga, the Bene Gesserit regroup on their secret stronghold world. There, they must confront a powerful new enemy, safeguard their millennia-old knowledge, and perhaps forge a new path for the survival of their order—and humanity itself. A conclusion brimming with intrigue and opening doors to the unknown.

All six books maintain a shared spirit, though each possesses its own distinct tone—from the heroic saga of the first Dune to the mythic scale of God Emperor. Herbert's works not only earned passionate acclaim from fans but achieved remarkable commercial success: the Dune novels were among the first science fiction works to reach bestseller status both in the U.S. and internationally. Notably, Children of Dune became the first sci-fi novel to top The New York Times bestseller list—proving that complex, "intelligent" science fiction could have mass appeal.

The Expanded Universe: New Chapters of Legacy

After Frank Herbert's death in 1986, his son, Brian Herbert, and author Kevin J. Anderson continued the saga. Drawing on Frank's notes, drafts, and outlines, they wrote dozens of books—prequels, side stories, and two volumes intended to conclude the original cycle: Hunters of Dune and Sandworms of Dune.

These texts delve deeply into the lore of the universe, exploring:

- ✦ The Butlerian Jihad
- ✦ The formation of the Spacing Guild and Bene Gesserit
- ✦ The rise of House Harkonnen and House Atreides

Entire arcs were developed around the Tleilaxu, the Great Schools, and far-flung worlds. The lore undeniably grew broader. But with it came a division of perception.

To some, the newer books represent development, structure, and a chance to revisit the universe. To others, they signal a tonal shift: more action, direct exposition, and clear-cut morality—less subtext, philosophy, and ambiguity.

Nevertheless, these books ensured that Dune never faded into the archives. It continues to be read, discussed, adapted. And even if readers across the saga's many "layers" don't always agree—that, too, is part of a living world's life.

But how does a reader navigate this ever-growing constellation of books and eras?

Chapter 3. How to Read Dune?

> « *Seek freedom and become captive of your desires. Seek discipline and find your liberty* » — *Muad'Dib*

Stepping into the world of Dune can at first feel like walking into a desert without a map. But fear not, traveler! Your efforts will be rewarded with entry into one of the most intricately crafted and influential universes in the history of science fiction. This chapter is your compass — helping you chart a course through the sands of time and the books of the Dune saga.

The Foundation of the Saga

As we've already seen, the undisputed heart and canon of the universe lies in the six novels written by its creator, Frank Herbert:

1. Dune (1965)
2. Dune Messiah (1969)
3. Children of Dune (1976)
4. God Emperor of Dune (1981)
5. Heretics of Dune (1984)
6. Chapterhouse Dune (1985)

The vast majority of experienced readers and critics agree: your journey should begin with the first book — Dune (1965). This is the most reliable and coherent way to absorb Herbert's vision. Following this path allows you to:

✦ Witness the development of the world and its characters exactly as the author intended.

✦ Gradually immerse yourself in increasingly complex philosophical and political ideas.

✦ *Feel the narrative scale expand* — from the fate of a planet to that of an entire species.

For the Experienced Traveler

There is another way — reading the saga in chronological order of events. This route is ideal for those already familiar with the core narrative and who now wish to experience it through the lens of in-universe history.

Warning: This path is not recommended for newcomers. It reveals secrets that Herbert intentionally concealed and structured across his original arc.

But for those already steeped in the saga and curious to follow the grand chronology (or who simply love reading in-universe timelines), here's a suggested reading order of the major novels. (Expanded Universe books are marked [EU]).

1. The Age of the Butlerian Jihad and the Founding of the Schools (Ancient History):

The Legends of Dune Trilogy [EU]:

✦ *The Butlerian Jihad* — the start of the great war against thinking machines.

✦ *The Machine Crusade* — the continuation of the brutal conflict across the galaxy.

✦ *The Battle of Corrin* — the final confrontation that reshaped the universe.

The Great Schools of Dune Trilogy [EU]:

✦ *Sisterhood of Dune* — the origins and rise of the Bene Gesserit order.

✦ *Mentats of Dune* — the foundation of the Mentat school of thought.

✦ *Navigators of Dune* — the story of the first Guild Navigators and their transformation.

2. The Era Before Dune (Recent Past):

The Prelude to Dune Trilogy [EU]:

✦ *House Atreides* — the story of young Leto and his ascension.

- *House Harkonnen* — explores the schemes and cruelty of Baron Harkonnen.

- *House Corrino* — details the political intrigue of Emperor Shaddam IV.

The Caladan Trilogy [EU]:

- *The Duke of Caladan* — centers on Duke Leto facing an impossible choice between his people and a new, perilous duty for the Imperium.

- *The Lady of Caladan* — explores Lady Jessica's torn loyalties between the Bene Gesserit's secret plans and her love for Duke Leto and Paul.

- *The Heir of Caladan* — follows young Paul Atreides as he navigates his training, confronts rising threats, and takes his first steps toward his monumental destiny.

Standalone [EU]:

- *Princess of Dune* — focusing on Irulan during this period.

3. The Era of Paul Muad'Dib (Core Saga and Interquels):

- *Dune* — Frank Herbert (Core Canon)
- *Paul of Dune [EU]* — set partially during and after Dune
- *Dune Messiah* — Frank Herbert (Core Canon)
- *The Winds of Dune [EU]* — bridges Dune Messiah and Children of Dune, focusing on Lady Jessica
- *Children of Dune* — Frank Herbert (Core Canon)

4. The Age of the God Emperor and the Millennia Beyond (Core Saga):

- *God Emperor of Dune* — Frank Herbert (Core Canon)
- *Heretics of Dune* — Frank Herbert (Core Canon)
- *Chapterhouse: Dune* — Frank Herbert (Core Canon)

5. The Conclusion of the Saga (Based on Frank Herbert's Notes):

- *Hunters of Dune [EU]* — continues the story from Chapterhouse: Dune, following the fugitive crew of a no-ship as they are hunted across the galaxy by a mysterious new enemy.
- *Sandworms of Dune [EU]* — concludes the original saga, where the mysteries and conflicts built across the series reach their climax in a final, universe-spanning confrontation.

Minor Oases: Short Stories

A number of short stories in the Dune universe — primarily written by Brian Herbert and Kevin J. Anderson — are available as supplements to the novels. They are mostly compiled in Tales of Dune or published alongside Expanded Universe novels. While not essential to understanding the core saga, they offer enriching details and intimate glimpses into the world of Dune, especially for those who wish to dive deeper after finishing the major works.

1. The Butlerian Jihad Era:

- *Hunting Harkonnens* — early years of the Jihad.
- *Whipping Mek* — a tale from the machine war.
- *The Faces of a Martyr* — character-driven piece from the Jihad.
- *Red Plague* — A story of a biological threat during the Jihad.

2. The Era Before Dune:

- *Imperial Blood* — set during the reign of Emperor Elrood IX.

✦   *A Whisper of Caladan Seas* — takes place during the events of House Atreides.

3. The Original Dune Timeline:

✦   *The Edge of a Crysknife* — likely set during Paul's early days on Arrakis.

✦   *The Waters of Kanly* — follows Gurney Halleck.

✦   *Blood of the Sardaukar* — parallel to the events of the first novel.

4. The Dune Messiah Era and Beyond:

✦   *Sea Child* — explores the legacy of Liet-Kynes.

✦   *Treasure in the Sand* — thematically connected to Paul of Dune.

5. The Heretics of Dune Era:

✦   *Wedding Silk* — set during the time of Heretics of Dune.

Final Advice Before Departure

Don't rush — savor the details (see Chapter 1). Don't hesitate to consult this book's glossary (Chapter 5) if you come across unfamiliar terms. Reading Dune is not just a story — it's an experience that stays with the reader long after the last page.

The first step into the sands is made. The history is explored. The path is charted.

The next part of the book will be your guide to the universe itself: the structures, the orders, the terminology, the ecology.

We begin with the Imperium.

Forward.

PART II: THE WORLD AND ITS RULES

If Part I showed how Dune came to be and what it became, then Part II is your practical guide: here you'll learn how the Imperium works, who rules the known universe, and what forces shape the course of its history.

Chapter 4: The Great Houses

> « Governments, if they endure, always tend increasingly toward aristocratic forms. No government in history has been known to evade this pattern. » — *Politics as Repeat Phenomenon, Bene Gesserit Training Manual*

The Galactic Imperium in the Dune universe is not a monolithic state but a complex feudal system that has lasted for ten thousand years. At its head sits the Emperor of House Corrino, enthroned on the Golden Lion Throne—but his power is far from absolute. It is counterbalanced by the might of the united Great Houses, represented in a council known as the Landsraad (for this and other terms, see Chapter 5), and by the empire's critical dependence on the Spacing Guild, which monopolizes interstellar travel.

The Great Houses are the pillars of the Landsraad—powerful aristocratic families that rule over entire planets or even star systems as their feudal fiefs. Their wealth and influence are often linked to their shares in the CHOAM Corporation (Combine Honnete Ober Advancer Mercantiles), the imperial economic megaconglomerate that controls the most vital trade and resources in the universe.

Life among the Great Houses is a never-ending game poised between war and diplomacy. Alliances are made, betrayals are plotted, and wars—both open and covert—are waged within the bounds of a strict code of honor, such as the ritualized vendetta known as kanly. The balance of power is fragile, and the struggle for dominance, resources (especially the invaluable spice of Arrakis), and prestige never ends. It is within this seething cauldron of ambition, honor, and treachery that the story of Dune unfolds.

Let's meet the key players of this galactic drama.

House Atreides

Values and Reputation: Honor, justice, loyalty to one's word and subjects—these are the principles for which House Atreides is renowned. Their nobility is widely acknowledged, though some consider it naïve in the brutal world of the Imperium. The Atreides value competence, bravery, and command the genuine love and loyalty of their people. Their military strength lies not in oppression but in discipline and high morale. According to legend, they trace their lineage back to the ancient heroes of Old Earth—the Atreidae (King Atreus and his son Agamemnon)—a mythic legacy that underscores the tragic grandeur running through their history.

History (Brief Summary): One of the oldest Great Houses, with a lineage spanning millennia. The Atreides have always held a respected position in the Landsraad, even if not among the wealthiest. Just before the events of the saga begin, the Emperor orders them to leave their ancestral world of Caladan and take control of the desert planet Arrakis, previously ruled by their mortal enemies—the Harkonnens.

Heraldry: A red hawk on a green-and-black field, symbolizing the nobility and courage of the house.

Home Planet: Caladan (see Chapter 7 for more information on the planets mentioned).

House Harkonnen

Values and Reputation: The antithesis of the Atreides. House Harkonnen is infamous for its cruelty, cunning, greed, and pathological brutality. Power is their sole objective, achieved through fear, torture, treachery, and ruthless economic exploitation. They scorn weakness and sentiment, relying instead on brute force, espionage, and manipulation. Their reputation in the Landsraad is grim, but their vast wealth and influence demand respect—even fear.

History (Brief Summary): Also an ancient House, whose rise is often associated with calculated ruthlessness and the elimination of rivals. The Harkonnens have nursed a blood feud with House Atreides for centuries.

They governed Arrakis for a long time as a quasi-fiefdom, extracting immense profits from spice production while violently suppressing the native Fremen population. The Emperor's decision to transfer control of Arrakis to the Atreides sets the stage for yet another of their dark plots.

Heraldry: A blue griffin—this mythical creature embodies ferocity, strength, and predation, perfectly reflecting the nature of the House.

Home Planet: Giedi Prime.

House Corrino

Role and Status: For ten thousand years, House Corrino has ruled the galaxy as the Imperial dynasty. Its members have borne the title of Padishah Emperor and are considered suzerains over all other worlds. Their greatest strength lies in the terrifying Sardaukar legions—elite troops fanatically loyal to the throne and feared across the Imperium.

Values and Reputation: Their primary goal is the preservation of imperial power and "stability"—as they define it. The Corrinos are masters of political intrigue, navigating the delicate balance between the Great Houses, the Landsraad, and the Spacing Guild. Their long reign has led to a degree of decadence and moral decay at court, but the authority of the throne and the might of the Sardaukar remain formidable.

History (Brief Summary): The dynasty rose to power after the Battle of Corrin, which ended the Butlerian Jihad against thinking machines (though the details of this are vague in the original saga; see the Expanded Universe for more). Since then, the Corrinos have ruled unchallenged. By the start of Dune, the reigning Emperor is Shaddam IV, who faces growing threats to his dominance—especially from House Atreides. Shaddam is portrayed as a capable yet vain ruler who tolerates no rivals.

Heraldry: The golden lion that adorns the throne of the Padishah Emperors is a classic symbol of kingship, strength, justice, and dominion — though justice has not always been evident in their rule.

Key Planets:

- *Kaitain:* The luxurious, prosperous capital of the Imperium and center of galactic politics and court life.

- *Salusa Secundus:* A harsh prison world with extreme conditions. It is here that the invincible Sardaukar are secretly trained; the brutal nature of Salusa forges their deadly prowess.

House Fenring

Formally a Minor House with no significant planetary holdings or military strength, House Fenring nonetheless wielded enormous covert influence within the Imperium—thanks largely to the unique position of Count Hasimir Fenring. A childhood friend of Emperor Shaddam IV, Fenring served as his most trusted agent and was often dispatched for covert missions involving espionage and assassination. His marriage to Lady Margot of the Bene Gesserit (see Chapter 7) further cemented their strategic position. Though lacking visible power, the Fenrings inspired both fear and respect at court, their name synonymous with mastery of political games behind the scenes.

Notable Houses from the Expanded Universe (Briefly)

[For new readers]: These Houses play important roles in the prequel novels set long before the events of Dune. They are not essential to understanding Frank Herbert's first novel and can be skipped on your first read. Feel free to return to this section if you choose to explore the Expanded Universe:

- *House Vernius*: Rulers of Ix, known for their advanced technology and complex machines (often skirting the limits of legality after the Butlerian Jihad). Allies of House Atreides and rivals to House Richese.

- *House Richese*: Another technologically advanced House and a long-standing competitor of Ix in innovation. Their fate is entwined with the political intrigues of the Imperium in the era leading up to Dune.

✦ *House Ecaz*: Lords of the lush planet Ecaz, famed for its exotic plants (notably the rare and valuable fogwood) and luxury goods. Ecaz played a notable role in Landsraad politics in the decades before House Atreides' move to Arrakis.

✦ *House Ginaz*: Less a political power and more a legendary martial tradition. The planet Ginaz is home to the Swordmasters, whose skill in combat is unmatched across the Imperium.

✦ *House Moritani*: A warlike House from Grumman, infamous for its ruthlessness, reliance on mercenaries, and long-standing feud with House Ecaz in the pre-Dune era.

✦ *House Tuek*: A powerful merchant family with deep ties to Arrakis. Long before the Atreides arrived, they were key players in Arrakis politics and maintained considerable influence over spice extraction and smuggling networks.

Behind every dynasty lies a system of values. Behind every banner—a political agenda. And behind every intrigue—a question: Who will control Arrakis?

To truly understand what's at stake, you must learn the language of the Imperium. In the next chapter, you'll find everything you need to navigate the terminology of Dune without getting lost.

Chapter 5: The Desert Speaks — Key Terms

« *The beginning of knowledge is the discovery of something we do not understand.* » — *Heretics of Dune*

Frank Herbert crafted a rich lexicon of terms and concepts that have become inseparable from the atmosphere and philosophical depth of his saga.

To help you navigate this world without getting lost in unfamiliar language, I've compiled this glossary. It does not claim to be exhaustive—more detailed term lists can often be found in the appendices of Herbert's original novels. My goal is to explain the essential words and ideas most critical for understanding the plot, culture, and worldview of Dune, and which appear frequently in the saga itself and throughout this guidebook.

Think of this as the language spoken by the desert itself—and by those who call it home. The entries are arranged alphabetically for your convenience.

A

Arrakis (Dune) — A desert planet, the third world in the Canopus system; the only known source of Spice (Melange), and the native world of the Fremen and Sandworms (see Chapter 8).

Atomics — Nuclear weapons held in the arsenals of the Great Houses, forbidden for use against humans under the Great Convention (see Chapter 9).

Axlotl Tank — A biological vat developed by the Bene Tleilax, used for growing gholas.

B

Bene Gesserit — An ancient sisterhood that secretly shapes Imperial politics through intrigue, a selective breeding program (aimed at creating the Kwisatz Haderach), and unique psycho-physical training (see Chapter 7).

Bene Tleilax — A closed society of fanatical genetic masters from the planet Tleilax; creators of gholas and Face Dancers.

Butlerian Jihad — An ancient crusade against thinking machines and AI, which established the long-standing ban on such technologies in the Imperium.

C

Carryall — A massive aerial transport vehicle used on Arrakis to carry or evacuate Harvesters.

CHOAM (Combine Honnete Ober Advancer Mercantiles) — The pan-Imperial trade and economic directorate that controls key resources; the wealth of the Houses largely depends on their shares in CHOAM.

Crysknife — A sacred Fremen blade made from the tooth of a Sandworm. It must be blooded before it can return to its sheath.

Cymeks — Historical figures (pre-Jihad): people whose brains were implanted into mechanical bodies.

D

Distrans — A device (often biological) used to transmit hidden mental messages.

E

Eyes of Ibad — Deep blue-within-blue eyes (without visible whites or pupils), signifying prolonged exposure to and dependency on Spice.

F

Face Dancer — A Bene Tleilax operative capable of changing their appearance to imitate others; the perfect spy or assassin.

Fedaykin — Elite Fremen warriors fanatically loyal to Muad'Dib, forming his personal guard and executing missions of holy war or vengeance.

Fremen — The native inhabitants of Arrakis' deserts, descendants of Zensunni Wanderers, perfectly adapted to the planet's harsh conditions.

G

Ghola — A clone grown in an Axlotl Tank by the Bene Tleilax from the cells of a deceased individual.

Glowglobe — A levitating light source powered by suspensors.

Golden Path — The philosophical and political vision of Leto II Atreides, intended to ensure the long-term survival of humanity.

Gom Jabbar — Often interpreted as "the enemy of arrogance"; a needle tipped with meta-cyanide poison. Used by the Bene Gesserit in a deadly test of humanity that challenges the subject to overcome base instincts with rational self-control.

Great Convention — The foundational legal code of the Imperium, guaranteeing a truce among Houses and banning the use of atomics against human targets.

Guild Navigator — A member of the Spacing Guild, mutated by Spice consumption to gain limited prescience, enabling them to navigate Heighliners through folded space.

H

Harvester (Crawler) — A giant machine used to collect Spice from the sands of Arrakis (see Chapter 6).

Heighliner — A massive interstellar transport ship operated by the Spacing Guild, using Holtzman engines to fold space (see Chapter 8).

Holtzman Effect — A scientific principle (named after Tio Holtzman) underpinning force shields, suspensors, and Heighliner drives (see Chapter 8).

Holtzman Shield — A personal or stationary force field that blocks fast-moving objects but lets slow ones pass through; attracts sandworms on Arrakis and explodes on contact with a lasgun (see Chapter 8).

Hunter-Seeker — A tiny airborne assassination device, guided by an operator.

I

Imperial Conditioning — Deep psychological training (notably for Suk Doctors) that theoretically renders one incapable of betrayal or harming designated individuals (e.g., a patient).

Imperium — The galactic human empire, governed by the Padishah Emperor and the Landsraad.

J

Jihad — A holy war. Typically refers to either the Butlerian Jihad or the Fremen Jihad under the banner of Muad'Dib.

K

Kanly — A formal vendetta or war between Great Houses, governed by the rules of the Great Convention.

Kwisatz Haderach — "Shortening of the Way" or "The one who can be many places at once"; the intended result of the Bene Gesserit breeding program—a male with their powers who can access ancestral memory on both the male and female lines.

L

Landsraad — The council of all Great Houses of the Imperium, serving as a legislative body and counterbalance to the Emperor's power.

Lasgun — A standard energy beam weapon used in the Imperium.

V

Verite / Will Rachine — Truth-inducing drugs used by the Bene Gesserit (especially Truthsayers). A crucial part of their toolkit.

Voice — The Bene Gesserit ability to control others through subtle modulation of speech.

M

Mahdi — "The one who will lead us to paradise"; a messianic figure from Fremen prophecy.

Maker (Shai-Hulud) — The Fremen name for the Sandworms, revered as desert deities.

Melange (Spice) — A unique psychoactive geriatric substance found only on Arrakis. Extends life, enhances consciousness (sometimes enabling prescience), causes intense addiction, and is vital to Guild Navigators (see Chapter 6).

Mentat — A human trained to function as a living computer; masters of logic, analysis, and strategy who replace banned AIs.

Missionaria Protectiva — A Bene Gesserit program of "planting" myths, prophecies, and religious beliefs across the galaxy for future manipulation by their agents.

O

Orange Catholic Bible (OCB) — The central religious text of the Imperium, created after the Butlerian Jihad and embodying its core commandments (including the ban on thinking machines).

Ornithopter (Thopter) — A flying vehicle for atmospheric travel, using flapping wings for lift and maneuverability.

Other Memory — The ability of Bene Gesserit Reverend Mothers (and some others) to access the ancestral memories of their female line.

P

Padishah Emperor — The formal title of the supreme ruler of the Imperium from House Corrino.

Poison Snooper — A device for detecting toxins in food or air, commonly used by the nobility.

Prana-Bindu — The Bene Gesserit discipline of nerve and muscle control, granting complete mastery of the body.

R

Reverend Mother — A high-ranking Bene Gesserit woman who has undergone the Spice Agony and gained access to ancestral memory.

S

Sandtrout — A flat, amoeba-like creature; the larval stage of the Sandworm. Encapsulates water and initiates the Spice cycle, contributing to the desertification of Arrakis.

Sardaukar — The Padishah Emperor's elite, fanatically loyal soldiers, their formidable combat skill forged by the brutal conditions of their home/training world, Salusa Secundus.

Sayyadina — Among the Fremen, a spiritual leader and acolyte who serves the tribe in religious matters and may undergo the Spice Agony to become a Reverend Mother.

Sietch — A Fremen settlement and refuge, typically carved into the rock formations of Arrakis.

Siridar — The official title of an Imperial planetary governor, ruler of a world or system granted as a fief to a Great or Minor House.

Solari — The standard currency of the Imperium, widely accepted for interstellar trade and CHOAM dealings; considered stable for millennia.

Stillsuit — A fitted Fremen survival suit designed to recover and recycle all bodily fluids into drinkable water.

Suk Doctor / Suk School — Graduates of the prestigious Suk School of Medicine, subjected to "Imperial Conditioning" (in theory) to make them incapable of harming a patient. Considered the most trusted physicians in the Imperium.

Suspensor — A Holtzman-based device that generates antigravity fields, allowing objects to levitate.

W

Water of Life — The "Poison of Awareness"; a concentrated, luminous blue liquid derived from the death of a juvenile Sandworm. It is created when the young worm is drowned in water — a fatal act that triggers a profound biochemical reaction. The resulting substance, essentially the worm's final exhalation, is saturated with highly refined Spice. Used in the Spice Agony ritual by both the Bene Gesserit and the Fremen, it unlocks ancestral memories and expanded perception. Surviving its effects is a transformative trial, marking the initiate as a Reverend Mother.

Weirding Way — The Bene Gesserit martial art based on Prana-Bindu disciplines; allows for extraordinary speed and precision in combat.

Z

Zensunni — A religious sect formed in ancient times from the fusion of Zen Buddhism and Sunni Islam. The Zensunni Wanderers, persecuted for their beliefs, migrated across the galaxy for millennia until their descendants settled on Arrakis, becoming the Fremen. Their teachings and history are foundational to Fremen culture and faith.

Understanding these terms is the key to a deeper appreciation of the universe and the complex forces that drive its history.

Now, armed with this knowledge, we can continue our journey through the Pillars of the Imperium and turn to its most valuable treasure...

Chapter 6: The Spice Must Flow

« *He who controls the spice controls the universe.* » — *Baron Harkonnen*

If the universe of Dune has a center—a point around which all intrigues, wars, and destinies revolve—it is, without question, Melange, more commonly known as the Spice. It is the most mysterious, the most valuable, and the most dangerous substance in the Known Universe. It's no coincidence that the maxim which defines the politics and economy of the Imperium for millennia is: "The Spice Must Flow."

To understand Melange is to touch the pulse of the Dune universe—its wars, its religions, its transformations.

What Is It? Origin and Nature

Visually, Melange appears as a fine powder or crystalline substance of orange-brown hue. Its most distinctive trait is its intense but pleasant aroma, reminiscent of cinnamon—though the true bouquet of its scent and flavor is far more complex and unique.

The most astonishing aspect of Melange lies in its origin. It can be found on only one planet in the vast expanse of the universe—the sun-scorched desert world of Arrakis, also known as Dune. All attempts to artificially synthesize Spice or to locate viable analogs on other planets have failed—often catastrophically.

Melange is not mined like conventional ore. It is an organic product of a uniquely complex symbiosis and is inextricably linked to the giant Sandworms. Spice is typically harvested after a so-called spice blow—a violent subterranean event in which a pre-melange mass erupts, blasting tons of mature Spice mixed with sand onto the surface.

Spice harvesting is a complex and highly dangerous industrial operation. At its core are massive machines known as Harvesters or Spice Crawlers. These monstrous, tracked mobile factories crawl slowly across the sand seas, devouring dunes with their rotary scoops in search of those precious orange grains. Inside the Harvester, the Spice is separated from useless sand and dust, and the spent matter is discarded back into the desert.

But all this industrial power is merely a fragile shell in the face of the desert's true master. The monotonous, rhythmic operation of the machinery—and the vibration of treads—inevitably, like the beat of a war drum, draws the attention of Shai-Hulud from the deep sands. Thus, Harvester operations are always a race against time and fraught with danger. The crew relies entirely on spotter ornithopters circling overhead, watching for the telltale sign of a worm approaching—the worm sign in the sand. Once danger is confirmed, the Harvester must be immediately airlifted by a massive transport aircraft—a Carryall. Only a Carryall is large and fast enough to lift the multi-ton Harvester to safety before the gaping maw of the Maker opens beneath it.

The Life Cycle of the Sandworms and Their Connection to Spice

The origin of Spice is inextricably linked to the astonishing life cycle of Arrakis's only truly native lifeforms—the giant Sandworms, known to the Fremen as Shai-Hulud, or the Makers. This cycle remains one of the most closely guarded secrets in the Dune universe:

1. *Sandtrout* — The earliest stage of the worm's life. These are small, flat, leathery, diamond-shaped organisms. The Fremen call them water-stealers. Sandtrout instinctively seek out and encapsulate any trace of water deep beneath the sands, sealing it off from the surrounding environment. This trait is what transformed Arrakis into a desert world.

2. *Pre-Spice Mass* — Within these sealed pockets of water, complex biochemical processes begin. The waste products of the sandtrout react with the water, forming a fungal-like culture that grows and eventually transforms into an unstable pre-spice mass.

3. *Spice Blow* — As pressure builds within the pre-spice mass, it eventually detonates in a powerful underground explosion. This spice blow violently scatters vast amounts of mature Melange across the desert surface, along with spores of the sandtrout. Most of the trout perish in the process.

4. *Little Maker* — The surviving sandtrout spores, if they find favorable conditions (especially an environment free of water), begin to develop into small Sandworms.

5. *Shai-Hulud* — Over centuries, these juvenile worms grow into colossal beings hundreds of meters long. They rule the desert, produce oxygen for Arrakis's sparse atmosphere, and fiercely defend

their territory, reacting to any rhythmic vibrations on the sand's surface. It is these great worms that make Spice harvesting a deadly endeavor. To the Fremen, Shai-Hulud is a sacred creature—an incarnation of the desert god.

A crucial point in this cycle is the fact that water is a lethal poison to all stages of the worm's life, from sandtrout to full-grown Shai-Hulud. This explains not only the arid climate of Arrakis but also the unique biochemistry behind the formation of Spice.

The Effects of Melange: Gift and Curse

The impact of Spice on the human body is complex and multifaceted, varying with dosage and individual predisposition:

1. *Geriatric Properties (Longevity)*: The most widely known and accessible effect of melange is significant life extension. Regular consumption slows the aging process and can grant centuries of active life. This makes Spice highly coveted by the wealthy and powerful throughout the Imperium.

2. *Expanded Consciousness and Prescience*: This is the most important and mysterious effect. In certain individuals—especially those exposed to large doses or refined forms—melange awakens latent abilities of prescience: the capacity to perceive probable futures. This property is critically important to:

    • *Spacing Guild Navigators*: They live immersed in tanks filled with concentrated Spice gas, which mutates their bodies and grants them the ability to see safe paths through folded space-time. Without Navigators, interstellar travel becomes impossible—and the entire Imperium would collapse.

    • *Bene Gesserit Reverend Mothers*: Spice is used in the perilous ritual known as the Spice Agony, unlocking genetic memory (Other Memory) and bestowing limited prophetic insight.

- *Fremen*: Constant exposure to Spice through food, water, and the very air of Arrakis stains the sclera and irises of their eyes a deep blue—the Eyes of Ibad. It also enhances their endurance, sharpens the senses, and may grant them subtle flashes of intuitive foresight.

3. *Addiction*: Melange induces powerful physical and psychological dependency. Once addiction takes hold, withdrawal is fatal—there is no known cure. This renders everyone who becomes dependent—from the Emperor to the lowest laborer on Arrakis—a hostage to Spice. The blue Eyes of Ibad are an unmistakable marker of this dependence.

Why Melange Is the Key to the Universe

The significance of Spice is absolute—it cannot be overstated. It is the axis upon which the entire civilization of the Imperium turns:

- *Interstellar Travel*: Without Spice, there are no Guild Navigators. Without them, there is no trade, no communication between worlds, no movement of armies—no Empire.

- *Political Power*: Control over Arrakis—the sole source of Spice—means unimaginable power. Whoever controls the Spice controls the Spacing Guild, influences the Emperor and the Landsraad, and holds the economy and fate of the galaxy in their grasp. This is why Arrakis has been the battleground of the bloodiest wars and the most intricate intrigues.

- *Human Evolution*: Spice is both a catalyst and a symbol of humanity's potential—and its peril. Prescience, longevity, altered states of consciousness—all are tied to melange.

- *Economy*: It is the most valuable substance in the known universe. The entire CHOAM system is founded on the trade and distribution of Spice.

Conclusion

Melange is far more than a drug or a resource. It is the lifeblood of the Imperium, the key to space and time, a catalyst for human transformation—and the curse of addiction. It is a biological marvel, an economic foundation, a political weapon, and a near-religious icon.

Understanding its many facets is essential to comprehending the world of Dune—a world in which every grain of orange dust is paid for in blood, lives, and the destinies of civilizations.

This orange powder, like a gravity well, draws not only the Great Houses into its pull...

Chapter 7: Hidden Schools and Open Powers

« We Bene Gesserit sift people to find the humans. » — Lady Jessica

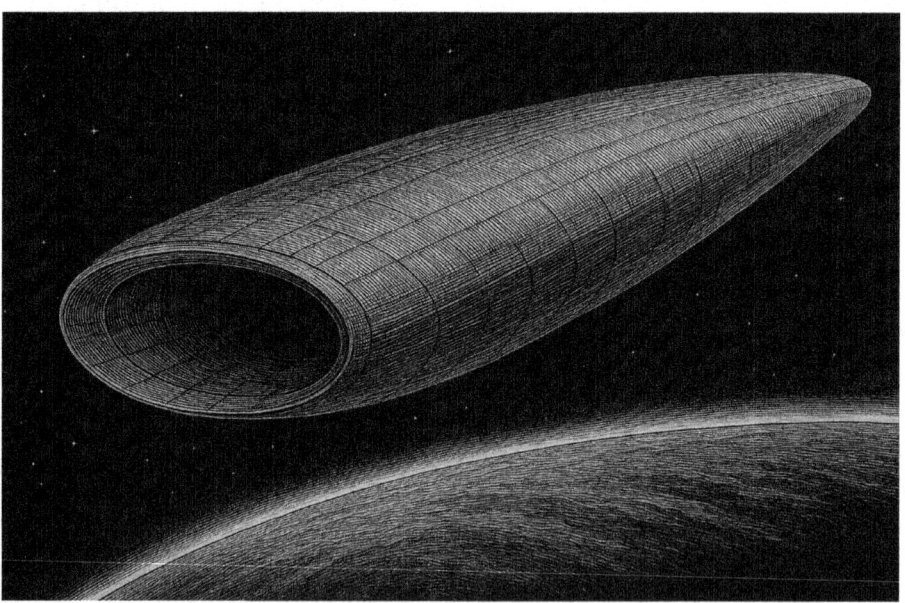

The political map of the Imperium is not only shaped by the power struggles of the Great Houses of the Landsraad and the authority of the Corrino Emperor. Over millennia, other powerful organizations have arisen in the universe of Dune, their influence rooted in secret knowledge, monopolies on essential services, or the subtle art of manipulation.

Bene Gesserit

Essence: An ancient, quasi-mystical sisterhood—an elite school of mental and physical mastery, open exclusively to women (with one legendary exception: the Kwisatz Haderach). Beneath their polished façades as advisors, courtiers, and spiritual guides lies a hidden agenda known only to the Sisterhood itself. It's no wonder they are commonly called "witches" for their uncanny powers and secrecy.

Goals: Their proclaimed mission is the service of humanity. In practice, this means guiding its chaotic evolution along a path the Sisterhood deems necessary for the species' survival. Their primary instrument is a selective breeding program, spanning thousands of years, with the ultimate aim of producing the Kwisatz Haderach—a male Bene Gesserit who can access ancestral memory on both male and female lines and perceive pathways through space and time.

Methods (Their arsenal is unmatched):

- *Prana-Bindu*: Supreme mastery over their own bodies—every muscle, nerve, and biochemical process.

- *The Voice*: The ability to control others through minute vocal modulations that act directly on the subconscious.

- *Observation and Analysis*: Extraordinary awareness and the ability to detect deception (the Truthsense). Many serve as Truthsayers to the Great Houses.

- *Genetic Program*: Carefully planned unions and lineages among noble Houses.

- *Missionaria Protectiva*: The Sisterhood's covert operation—seeding myths, prophecies, and religious beliefs on various planets to be activated by Bene Gesserit agents when needed.

+ *Spice Agony*: A dangerous ritual involving the "Water of Life" (a toxic derivative of Spice) that allows a successful initiate to become a Reverend Mother and access the Other Memory of her female ancestors.

Influence: Vast and far-reaching, though rarely public. Their acolytes become wives, concubines, and confidants of the most powerful men in the Imperium. Their breeding program touches nearly every noble bloodline. The Bene Gesserit play the long game—their strategies unfold over centuries.

Spacing Guild and Navigators

Essence: A powerful organization holding an absolute monopoly over all interstellar transport and banking operations within the Imperium. The Guild maintains strict political neutrality, allowing it to deal with all factions—Emperor, Landsraad, and Great Houses alike. Its influence is rooted in the unique abilities of its Navigators.

Goals: To preserve its monopoly on space travel at any cost. To ensure uninterrupted supplies of melange, without which the Navigators cannot function. To maintain a relative stability within the Imperium—necessary for commerce and transit. The Guild zealously guards the secrets of navigation and the true nature of its Navigators.

Methods:

+ *Heighliners*: Colossal spacefaring vessels capable of carrying entire fleets of Great House ships within their holds. They "fold" space using Holtzman generators, enabling near-instantaneous travel between star systems.

+ *Guild Navigators*: Individuals subjected from childhood to intense mutation through prolonged exposure to concentrated Spice gas. They live submerged in specialized tanks, their bodies grotesquely altered—enlarged craniums, atrophied limbs. Spice grants them limited prescience, allowing them to "see" safe paths through folded space and avoid gravitational traps. Without them, space travel is impossible.

> + *Neutrality and Secrecy*: The Guild does not interfere in House wars, offering transport to anyone who pays. All information regarding the Navigators and their needs is highly classified.

Influence: Utter and unquestioned. The Guild's control over travel gives it leverage no sword can match. A denial of transport can paralyze any House—or even the Emperor himself. Their utter dependence on Spice makes Arrakis the focal point of their long-term interests.

Order of Mentats

Essence: Humans specially trained to perform the functions of thinking machines. After the Butlerian Jihad and the ensuing ban on artificial intelligence, a need for individuals capable of performing complex logical calculations, data analysis, and strategic planning arose. Mentats are valued for their cold logic and ability to process vast amounts of information.

Goals: To achieve the highest possible efficiency of thought and provide accurate forecasts and strategic insights based on data analysis. The Order itself functions more as a training standard and a professional community than a unified political force. Mentats serve various Great Houses, the Emperor, or other organizations.

Methods:

> + *Mental Training*: Development of exceptional memory, observational skills, and pure logic from an early age.

> + *Data Analysis*: The ability to detect hidden patterns, probabilities, and consequences within streams of information.

> + *Logic Over Emotion (Ideally)*: A constant pursuit of objective conclusions, although Mentats remain human and subject to personal flaws. Some enhance their concentration with sapho juice.

Influence: In a world without computers, a Mentat is an invaluable asset. Their calculations and predictions underpin many of the political and military decisions made by the Great Houses. Having a skilled Mentat provides a significant advantage to any House.

Bene Tleilax

Essence: A closed, xenophobic society of fanatical geneticists from the planet Tleilax. They are unrivaled masters of biological engineering, though their technologies and ethical standards provoke revulsion and suspicion throughout the Imperium. Their true motives and long-term goals are buried beneath layers of secrecy and deception.

Goals: Beneath their public facade as genetic scientists lies a hidden religious agenda: to reshape the galaxy according to their beliefs, using biology as a tool for total control.

Methods:

- *Genetic Engineering*: The creation of "enhanced" humans, biological weapons, and tools.

- *Gholas*: Cloned duplicates of deceased individuals grown from their cells. The Tleilaxu possess the secret of memory restoration in gholas—though they keep this fact closely guarded.

- *Face Dancers*: Genderless humanoid shapeshifters capable of altering their appearance to imitate others, making them ideal spies and assassins.

- *Axlotl Tanks*: Mysterious biotechnology, presumably used to grow gholas and possibly other biological products, including synthetic melange (though the latter remains speculative and unconfirmed in the core saga).

- *Manipulation and Secrecy*: The Tleilaxu operate through front agents, misinformation, and deep-cover infiltration.

Influence: The Tleilaxu are suppliers of unique—and often forbidden—biotechnologies (gholas, Face Dancers) that others within the Imperium either need or secretly desire. Their mastery of flesh and gene renders them indispensable—and deeply feared. Few dare to trust them, yet fewer can afford not to. Whispers of Tleilaxu secrets haunt the corridors of power, where desire often overrides disgust.

Landsraad

Essence: An assembly of the Great Houses that formally serves as a counterbalance to the power of the Emperor.

Goals: To protect the collective interests and privileges of the aristocracy from imperial overreach or external threats. To maintain feudal equilibrium and settle disputes between Houses under the framework of the Great Convention, which regulates the rules of warfare and the use of certain weapons.

Methods: Political debate and voting in the High Council. Formation of alliances and coalitions. Collective security agreements. The power to declare war on an outlawed House. In theory, the ability to unite against the Emperor himself.

Influence: Though fractured and divided, the Landsraad holds true power in unity. It alone can depose the Emperor—if the Houses can agree among themselves.

Briefly: Other Powers

1. *Fish Speakers*: An all-female military force that rose to prominence in the later eras of the Imperium, especially during and after the 3,500-year reign of the God Emperor. Known for their unwavering loyalty to their divine ruler, they served as enforcers of his peace and became a dominant power in their own right.

2. *Smugglers*: An informal yet pervasive force, particularly on Arrakis. Specializing in illegal trade—most notably the clandestine export of Spice outside the control of the Great Houses and CHOAM. Operating outside the law, but often better informed than those within it.

Conclusion

These organizations reveal that true strength lies not merely in armies or wealth but in foresight, subtlety—and the patience to play the long game.

And like every game of power, there is always a board.

In the next chapter, we step onto that board—the key planets of the Imperium, where Great Houses and secret orders enact their grand designs. These worlds are not just the stage of conflict... but the very pieces and prizes of the game.

Chapter 8: The Known Universe – Key Worlds

« *The desert takes the weak.* » — *Fremen proverb*

The Imperium of Man spans thousands of star systems and an untold number of planets. Yet in the epic saga of Dune, only a handful of worlds play truly pivotal roles—shaping the course of history, forging the identities of its characters, and standing as centers of power or sources of vital resources. These planets are as varied as the cultures that inhabit them—from sun-blasted deserts and industrial hellscapes to oceanic havens and shining imperial capitals. Let us explore the most essential among them.

Seats of Power

1. Arrakis (also known as Dune)

Description and Climate: A desert world, the third planet in the Canopus system. Endless dunes, rocky outcroppings, searing heat, and an eternal scarcity of water define its landscape. Home to the giant Sandworms and saturated with the Spice, whose scent drifts through the very air. Arrakis is a trial, a crucible that mercilessly discards the weak and rewards only those who can adapt to its deadly conditions.

Significance: The most important planet in the universe. A paradox—barren, yet priceless. The sole known source of Melange, making it the ultimate prize in the galactic power struggle. Birthplace of the Fremen, a people perfectly adapted to the desert and inseparable from it. The main stage upon which the saga unfolds.

Control: Control: At the start of Dune, stewardship of Arrakis is transferred from House Harkonnen to House Atreides—a gift indistinguishable from a curse.

2. Caladan

Description and Climate: The fourth planet in the Delta Pavonis system. The antithesis of Arrakis—a world of abundant water, oceans, rivers, and frequent rainfall. Lush vegetation, fertile soil, and a temperate climate define its tranquil beauty.

Significance: The ancestral fief of House Atreides for 26 generations. Symbolizes their values, their connection to nature, and the peaceable style of governance they are forced to abandon. Caladan is known for exporting pundi rice and wine. An idyllic world that may have lulled House Atreides into a false sense of peace—before casting them into the harsh, unrelenting reality of the Imperium. The contrast between Caladan and Arrakis is one of the saga's key thematic currents.

Control: House Atreides.

3. Giedi Prime

Description and Climate: The third planet in the 36 Eri A system (Omicron-2 Eridani). Grim, overcrowded, and heavily industrialized. The sky is often choked with smog, sunlight barely piercing the haze. Nature has been all but eradicated—scorched for profit. Factories operate without pause; cities fester like wounds on the land. Gladiator arenas and slavery are commonplace. Architecture and social order reflect the Harkonnen ethos: total domination of nature and humanity alike.

Significance: The homeworld and seat of power for House Harkonnen. The source of their military-industrial might, forged through ruthless exploitation.

Control: House Harkonnen.

4. Kaitain

Description and Climate: A planet in the Alpha Boötis system (Arcturus). A splendid, possibly terraformed garden world. The official capital of the Imperium for millennia. Lavish cities, grand architecture, curated parks and landscapes. The heart of galactic bureaucracy and aristocratic life.

Significance: Residence of the Corrino Emperors and the seat of the Landsraad High Council. A symbol of imperial power and the heart of political life in the galaxy.

A façade polished to a gleam—but beneath the marble and silk lies the rust of intrigue.

Everything here is grand, yet nothing truly lives. Perhaps even the Emperors themselves are prisoners in a gilded cage.

Control: House Corrino (Imperial House).

5. Salusa Secundus

Description and Climate: The third planet of the Gamma Waiping system. Officially designated as the Imperium's prison world. In reality—a hell that breeds devils. A world not meant for habitation, only survival. Scars of ancient ruins—possibly from nuclear bombardment—mark the landscape. Temperatures swing to extremes, poisonous vapors fill the air, and deadly fauna stalk the terrain. Fewer than one in ten survives the trial of this world.

Significance: The secret forge of the Sardaukar. The Emperor Corrino's most terrifying and hidden resource. It is the planet's inhuman conditions that forge criminals into fanatical, near-invincible warriors. A throne upheld by agony beyond imagining.

Ironically, this wasteland was once the ancestral capital of House Corrino. Its true purpose remains one of the Imperium's darkest and most closely guarded secrets.

Control: House Corrino (Imperial House).

Worlds of Technology and Secrecy

1. Ix

Description and Climate: The ninth planet of the Alpha Eridani (Achenar) system. Physical details are scarce in the original saga, as the focus lies more on its function than its surface. It is believed to be a high-tech world of subterranean or enclosed factory-cities, where natural light has long given way to the cold glow of artificial illumination.

Significance: Ix is the Imperium's foremost hub of advanced technology—renowned for developing complex devices and machines that often hover on the edge of legality under the proscriptions of the Butlerian Jihad. It is the homeworld of House Vernius. Many key technologies (such as distrans devices) are said to originate from Ix.

Control: Technocratic guilds and industrial corporations; historically tied to House Vernius.

2. Richese

Description and Climate: The fourth planet of the Epsilon Eridani system. Like Ix, Richese is celebrated for its technological output, though it leans more toward pragmatic mass production rather than cutting-edge innovation.

Significance: Often seen as the eternal rival to Ix. Where Ix is the elite artisan workshop of the Imperium, Richese is the massive factory—focused on simplified, reliable, and practical versions of high-end devices. Their output is widely used across the galaxy.

Control: House Richese and affiliated dynasties of engineers and manufacturers.

3. Tleilax

Description and Climate: A secretive and isolated world in the star system of Thalim. The Tleilaxu guard their domain zealously, barring outsiders and shrouding their world in mystery. It is presumed to be densely populated, its surface dotted with vast genetic laboratories.

Significance: The stronghold of the Bene Tleilax—heretical masters of genetics and flesh. Tleilax is the source of gholas, Face Dancers, and other transgressive biotechnologies that push the limits of ethics and legality. It is a planet whose alien customs and secretive practices inspire dread and revulsion throughout the Imperium.

Control: Bene Tleilax.

4. Wallach IX

Description and Climate: The ninth planet of the Laoualaps system. Little is known about its physical characteristics, but it was likely chosen by the Bene Gesserit for its isolation or some specific, undisclosed qualities.

Significance: For most of Imperial history, Wallach IX served as the primary stronghold and Mother School of the Bene Gesserit Sisterhood—a center of training, genetic planning, and the safeguarding of the Order's deepest secrets.

Control: Bene Gesserit.

Historically Significant Worlds (Briefly)

1. Earth (Old Terra)

Significance: A ghost of the past—the cradle of humanity, long lost, forgotten, or deemed unfit for life by the time of the Imperium. Its legacy lingers only in ancient myths, languages, place names, and echoes in the genetic memory. It plays no active role in the saga's present—but its shadow remains.

2. Corrin

Significance: A victory that birthed a dynasty. Located in the Sigma Draconis system, Corrin was the site of the final triumph in the Butlerian Jihad—the great war against thinking machines. From this forge of history, House Corrino rose to claim the Imperial throne. It was here that the Imperium, as we know it, truly began.

Conclusion

These are but a few scattered jewels in the boundless galaxy of the Imperium. Yet it is these worlds that shape the very terrain on which the saga unfolds. Their environments, resources, and secrets are intimately entwined with the destinies of Houses and factions alike.

To survive across such wildly divergent worlds, traverse the void between them, and wage war for their riches, humanity was compelled to forge a unique technological path—a paradoxical fusion of the ultramodern and the archaic, born in the enduring shadow of the Butlerian Jihad.

Chapter 9: Machines and Men

> « Thou shalt not make a machine in the likeness of a human mind. » — Commandment from the Orange Catholic Bible

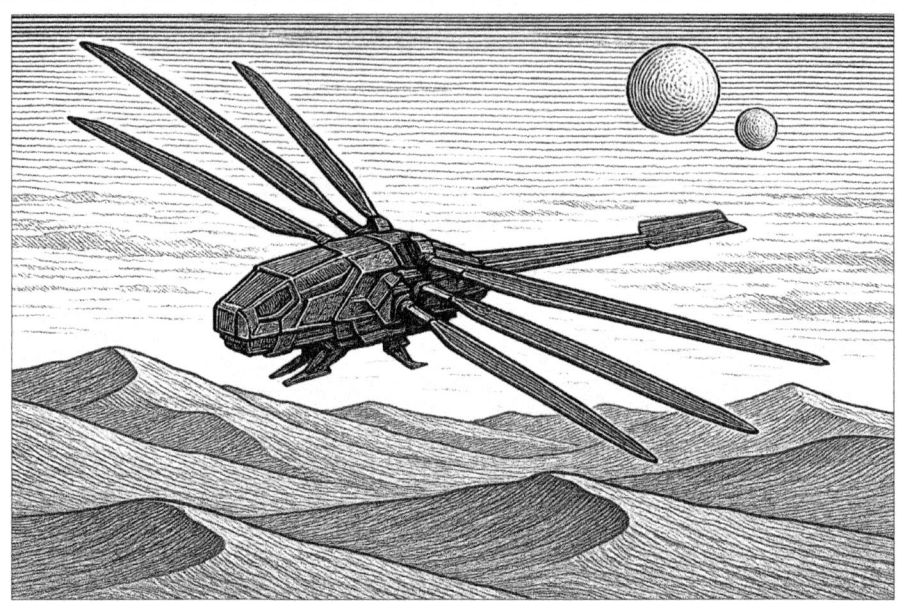

The technological landscape of Dune is both extraordinary and paradoxical. Humanity has conquered the stars, harnessed force fields, and manipulated genetics—yet has turned its back on thinking machines and artificial intelligence.

This rejection is the direct result of the Butlerian Jihad—a holy war against "thinking machines" that occurred ten thousand years before the events of the main saga and forever altered the trajectory of civilization.

The Ban on Thinking Machines and Its Consequences

The central dogma of the Orange Catholic Bible—"Thou shalt not make a machine in the likeness of a human mind"—is not a mere archaic law but a foundational religious principle of the Imperium. Its violation is punishable by death.

The Butlerian Jihad, which nearly led to humanity's extinction, left a deep scar on civilization. The resulting ban represents a conscious philosophical choice: to renounce the convenience and power of AI in favor of cultivating human potential—with all its risks and rewards.

Its consequences are far-reaching:

- *No Computers or AI:* The Imperium lacks complex computational systems capable of autonomous thought or decision-making.

- *The Rise of Enhanced Human Abilities:* Their role has been filled by humans trained in extraordinary disciplines: Mentats (living computers), Guild Navigators (who use Spice to access prescience), and the Bene Gesserit (with their intense mental and physical training).

- *Specialized Technologies:* Innovation has focused on tools that amplify human capacity or serve specific functions—without mimicking the mind.

The Holtzman Effect

At the heart of many of the Imperium's most remarkable—and permitted—technologies is the Holtzman Effect, named after its legendary discoverer Tio Holtzman, a pre-Jihad physicist. This phenomenon governs the manipulation of space-time and gravitational fields. The exact scientific principles are a closely guarded secret—especially by the Spacing Guild—but it's known that devices using Holtzman generators do not possess sentience and are thus exempt from the machine ban.

Key Holtzman-based technologies include:

- Personal shields, which repel fast-moving objects.

- Heighliner drives, which fold space for instantaneous travel.

- Suspensors, antigravity devices that allow objects to levitate - from floating glowglobes to the infamous Baron Harkonnen himself.

Thus, the legacy of Holtzman permeates the Imperium—quietly but profoundly shaping war, travel, and everyday existence.

Transportation

1. Thopters

The standard vehicle for atmospheric flight, ornithopters use beating wings—like birds or insects—to generate lift and maneuver. Their agility and ability to take off or land vertically make them ideal for reconnaissance, military operations, and everyday transport on varied worlds—from desert patrols on Arrakis to coastal flights over Caladan. Their distinctive buzzing or whirring has become part of the aural fabric of many worlds.

2. Carryall

If the ornithopter is the Imperium's versatile aerial transport, then the carryall is its massive airborne partner—designed for one critical task: the extraction and emergency evacuation of spice Harvesters on Arrakis.

This colossal flying craft (likely with vertical takeoff and landing capabilities) is equipped with powerful engines and specialized grappling mechanisms that allow it to lift the multi-ton spice crawler from the sands.

In the dangerous race against time—when Shai-Hulud is already surging toward a working Harvester—the lives of the crew and the salvation of unimaginably valuable equipment depend entirely on the speed and reliability of the carryall.

Without these airborne giants and their life-saving role, industrial spice harvesting on Dune would be nearly impossible.

3. Guild Heighliners

Colossal leviathans drifting through folded space—ships the size of cities, bearing fleets, legions, and merchant caravans in their vast steel bellies.

Using Holtzman drives to fold space, they enable near-instantaneous travel between star systems—made possible only through the prescient guidance of Guild Navigators.

Heighliners are not merely vessels; they are the Imperium's only bridge between stars.

Weapons and Defense

1. Lasguns

Directed-energy weapons that emit lethal beams of coherent light. Common in both personal and military use, lasguns are a standard armament across the Imperium.

2. Holtzman Shields

Personal (and sometimes stationary) force fields generated by Holtzman devices. Shields block fast-moving objects like bullets or lasgun beams but allow slow-moving items—such as the blade of a knife or an extended hand—to pass through. This has radically altered combat tactics, reviving the importance of hand-to-hand weapons. Shields are used in duels, security, and base defense—but are nearly useless on Arrakis, where they attract sandworms.

3. The Shield-Lasgun Interaction

A critically dangerous phenomenon. When a lasgun beam strikes a Holtzman shield, the result is an unpredictable pseudo-atomic explosion—often fatal to both parties and devastating to the surroundings. Due to this risk, using lasguns against shielded targets is considered highly dangerous and is forbidden by the rules of warfare (the Great Convention)—though such rules are sometimes broken.

4. Atomics

Nuclear weapons still exist in the arsenals of the Great Houses. Their use against human targets is strictly forbidden by the Great Convention.

Violating this taboo trigger collective retaliation by the entire Landsraad. Atomics are considered doomsday weapons—tools of deterrence or targeting infrastructure in scenarios of total war.

5. Stone Burner

A weapon of terrifying power and mysterious origin—its true nature is never fully revealed, though it may be linked to nuclear energy.

Capable of burning through nearly any material across vast distances, it emits a strange and deadly form of radiation known as J-radiation, which causes blindness and catastrophic tissue damage in living beings.

Feared even by those who wield it, the Stone Burner is used only rarely—its destructive power matched only by the peril it leaves behind.

Personal Equipment

1. Stillsuit

Arguably the most vital survival technology on Arrakis—and a symbol of Fremen adaptation. This form-fitting, multilayered suit functions as a highly efficient, portable system of filtration and water reclamation.

It captures nearly all moisture released by the body—including sweat, urine, and even breath—then channels it through intricate filtration units and returns it as drinking water via a tube near the chin.

The stillsuit's design, perfected over generations by the Fremen, allows for the loss of only the smallest fraction of precious moisture each day—making survival and travel through the most arid regions of the desert not only possible but sustainable.

Proper wearing, fitting, and maintenance of the suit are not merely matters of life and death—they are expressions of discipline, cultural identity, and reverence for water in Fremen society.

Biotechnologies

1. Gholas

A chilling genetic art practiced by the Bene Tleilax. A ghola is a clone, grown in an axlotl tank from the cells of a deceased organism. The Tleilaxu are capable of producing exact physical copies of the dead. (The full scope of ghola capabilities remains a closely guarded secret—and a key element of major storylines—thus, further details are withheld to avoid spoilers.)

2. Cymeks

Figures from a distant age—humans from the pre-Butlerian era who transplanted their brains into immortal mechanical bodies in pursuit of power and longevity. Often tyrants or generals, they came to symbolize the very threat that triggered the Jihad: the loss of humanity in the quest for domination through machines.

> Primarily featured in expanded universe materials, though the concept aligns with the thematic core of Frank Herbert's vision.

Communication and Espionage

1. Distrans Devices

Tools for covert communication, often biological in nature. These may be specially bred animals—such as birds or bats—genetically engineered to store and transmit mental messages.

The sender imprints a thought into the creature's nervous system; the receiver must use a specific mental cue or code phrase to retrieve it. It's a trusted method in environments where electronic communications risk interception. Frequently associated with Ixian technologies.

2. Nullentropy Beacons/Tubes

Devices that create a field in which time is effectively suspended. Used to preserve messages, samples, or even bodies indefinitely—without decay, degradation, or passage of time.

Conclusion

Frank Herbert's Imperium is a civilization where technology serves humanity—not the other way around. A society forever reshaped by the Butlerian Jihad, choosing introspection over automation, not progress for its own sake. This is one of Dune's central philosophical insights: It does not ask which technologies will save us— It asks who we become when we stop hiding behind them. In that question lies both the majesty and the fragility of the Imperium's path.

Chapter 10: The Fauna

« *The predator improves the stock.* » — Leto II

The galaxy settled by humanity teems with life—often as astonishing as it is dangerous. These pages gather knowledge of the living—knowledge sometimes as simple as a desert spoor, yet as valuable as a drop of water. Understanding the habits of a creature may mean not only an advantage—but survival itself. Special attention is given to the unmatched biosphere of Arrakis.

Identifier: Shai-Hulud

Taxonomy: Vermis giganticus arrakis. Local (Fremen) designations: The Maker, Old Man of the Desert, Grandfather of the Desert.

Habitat: Endemic to the planet Arrakis (Dune). Found exclusively in the open desert regions (ergs). Avoids rocky terrain and any form of free-standing water.

Morphology and Physiology: A colossal, segmented invertebrate, attaining lengths of several hundred meters (specimens exceeding 450m have been documented; legends speak even of kilometer-long specimens). The body is clad in thick, exceedingly strong armored plates, resistant to extreme temperatures and friction. Travels through the deep sands with tremendous velocity. Possesses a gigantic, tri-segmented maw ringed with thousands of crystalline teeth, suited for pulverizing rock and sand. Its metabolism is likely based on unexplored forms of chemosynthesis; excretes significant volumes of oxygen. Water is toxic.

Behavior: A highly territorial creature. Responds to rhythmic vibrations on the sand's surface as to a challenge or potential prey, surging inexorably toward the source, whether an incautious wayfarer or a giant harvester. Capable of engulfing large machinery. Moreover, for reasons that remain imperfectly understood (perhaps related to field harmonics or the peculiarities of Holtzman energy), the worms are inevitably and furiously drawn to active energy shields. Activating a personal shield in the open desert of Arrakis is tantamount to suicide, as it is guaranteed to provoke an attack by one or more Makers.

Other aspects of their behavior (reproduction, social structure) remain unstudied due to the extreme danger posed by the organism.

Ecological and Cultural Significance: The absolute apex predator and keystone species of the Arrakis ecosystem. Its life cycle is inextricably tied to the creation of the spice melange (see Chapter 6).

In Fremen culture, it occupies a sacred place—revered as a desert deity, a symbol of strength, eternity, and life itself on Dune. Its titanic power and ever-present danger shape all life on Arrakis, rendering spice harvesting a mortal gamble and elevating the worm to divine status among those who have embraced the ways of the desert.

The first encounter with Shai-Hulud is a profound shock: reverential awe before its elemental majesty and ancient might commingles with terror and the sense of utter insignificance before a power indifferent to Man, his dominion, or his entreaties.

Identifier: Sandtrout

Taxonomy: Aquaexus aramachus. Believed to be the larval or intermediate stage of Vermis giganticus arrakis.

Habitat: Ubiquitous within the sands of Arrakis, at various depths.

Morphology and Physiology: A small, flat, rhomboid creature roughly the size of a human palm, with no clearly defined external organs. Its body is leathery, flexible, and semi-permeable. It possesses a unique biological trait: the ability to encapsulate water.

Behavior: Exhibits pronounced negative hydrotropism—a tendency to seek out and isolate water. Massive congregations (or mergings) of sandtrout form natural barriers that trap moisture beneath the surface, a phenomenon believed to have contributed directly to the desertification of Arrakis.

Within these concealed water pockets, the sandtrout initiates a biochemical process that leads to the formation of pre-spice mass.

Ecological and Cultural Significance: An indispensable link in the Spice Cycle and the silent architect of Arrakis's barren terrain—its touch repels water and erases the very softness of the world. Critical to any understanding of Dune's ecology.

Other Endemic Species of Arrakis (Brief Notes)

Despite the sandworm's dominance, life on Arrakis includes other, more modest forms:

1. Desert Mouse (Muad'Dib)

(Mus Arrakis Adaptus): A small nocturnal rodent and a masterpiece of evolutionary adaptation. Capable of extracting moisture from even the most meager sources. For the Fremen, it symbolizes the wisdom of survival—its name carrying deep and layered meaning.

2. Bats

(Chiroptera arrakis spp): Various species of bats inhabiting natural caves and the deeper recesses of sietches. Integral to the planet's nocturnal ecosystem, likely preying on native insect life.

3. Arthropods

Diverse insects and arachnids which form the lower strata of the desert food chain. Dwelling most often near temporary oases.

Significance: Their disappearance is among the oldest signs of a worm's approach. The Fremen know: when a dune falls silent, Shai-Hulud soon rumbles beneath. These creatures may also serve as a last resort for sustenance in the deep desert.

Selected Faunal Representatives of Other Worlds

Beyond the unique ecosystem of Arrakis, the Imperium harbors other remarkable creatures worthy of note:

1. Laza Tiger (from Salusa Secundus)

Taxonomy (Presumed): Felis Laza Chameleon.

Description: A product of genetic engineering from the Old Imperium. Large predatory cats whose pelage shimmers like a mirage, enabling them nearly to merge with their environment or even—as Salusan legends assert—to project illusions for disorienting prey. Exceedingly aggressive and dangerous.

Significance: Employed as exotic guard beasts, instruments of the hunt, or tools of execution on Salusa Secundus and in the estates of certain Great Houses. Embodiments of engineered peril within the Imperium.

2. Salusan Bulls (from Salusa Secundus)

Taxonomy (Presumed): Bos Sanguinarius Salusae.

Description: Massive, highly aggressive, bull-like creatures, either bred or adapted to the harsh conditions of Salusa Secundus. Renowned for their uncontrollable fury.

Significance: Used in brutal gladiatorial contests—corridas—once popular among the Imperial nobility. To die at the horns of a Salusan bull in the arena was considered a twisted kind of valor, though often the inglorious fate of those ensnared by court intrigue—as in the case of Duke Leto's father.

3. Chairdog (from Tleilax)

Taxonomy (Presumed): Canis Lectularius Tleilaxu.

Description: A living organism, bio-engineered into an article of furniture. The Chairdog instinctively molds itself to the anatomy of the one seated, providing ideal comfort—one can only speculate whether it sometimes whimpers in its sleep.

Significance: A chilling testament to Tleilaxu mastery over living flesh. Blurring the boundary between organism and object of luxury, it reflects a morality alien to the rest of the Imperium—utilitarian, indifferent, and unsettling.

Conclusion

Other lifeforms of the Imperium fall outside the scope of this survey, as their mention bears less relevance to the primary saga and might overcomplicate this introductory overview.

The species presented here have been selected primarily for their iconic nature and their critical impact on the events of the universe.

PART III: CHARACTERS AND DEEP MEANING

Here, beyond the shifting dunes of narrative, something larger takes shape. We meet the gaze of those who bear the weight of galactic fate.

Who is Paul—victim, messiah, or instrument? Why did Leto II become a monster for the sake of the future?

We will explore not only actions but the philosophical forces behind them.

> This section explores the full arc of Frank Herbert's original six novels, from Dune to Chapterhouse: Dune. As such, it inevitably reveals major plot developments, character fates, critical outcomes, and secrets that unfold across the saga.
>
> If you have not yet completed the saga and want to preserve the experience of discovering it for yourself, I strongly recommend pausing here and first reading all six novels of Frank Herbert's original series.
>
> If you are preparing to start the saga now or returning to it with fresh eyes, the knowledge you gained from the first two parts of this guide will help you better understand the worlds, powers, and hidden structures that shape Dune's story.
>
> This part of the book will await your return—ready to offer reflection and a deeper dialogue with the universe of Dune once your path through the saga is complete.
>
> **Spoiler Alert: Heavy Spoilers Ahead!**

Chapter 11: House Atreides: The Burden of Honor and Destiny

The story of Dune begins with a House bound by honor—and burdened by it.

House Atreides stands as a beacon of nobility, loyalty, and vision in a universe ruled by fear, manipulation, and betrayal. Their lineage will shape the galaxy's fate for millennia to come.

Yet, in the harsh reality of Dune, nobility is not a shield but a blade that cuts both ways.

Let us turn to the key figures of this lineage...

1. Duke Leto I Atreides

Role and Significance: Head of House Atreides at the start of the saga, father of Paul. The embodiment of a noble leader—charismatic, just, devoted to his people, a skilled politician and warrior. His relocation to Arrakis under Imperial order sets in motion a chain of tragic events. Leto is a central figure in the first part of Dune, and his death becomes the launching point for Paul's tragic path.

Development and Fate: Leto is fully aware that the assignment to Arrakis is a trap orchestrated by the Emperor and House Harkonnen. He tries to turn the situation to his advantage, hoping to secure the support of the Fremen—the "desert power"—but underestimates the depth of betrayal (most notably in the person of Dr. Yueh).

He dies during the Harkonnen assault on Arrakeen, attempting in his final moments to kill the Baron with a poison capsule—but fails. The Baron survives, though wounded.

Leto remains in the memories of Paul and Jessica as a symbol of honor, duty, and the lost world of Caladan.

Core Traits: Nobility, justice, charisma, responsibility, insight (he recognizes the trap), tragic dignity, paternal love.

> *Voice (Quote)*: « *A man is tested at the moment of parting.* » *(Reflecting on the loyalty of his men before leaving Caladan).*

2. Lady Jessica

Role and Significance: Official concubine (though beloved as if a wife) of Duke Leto, mother of Paul and Alia. A Bene Gesserit adept who defied the Order's directive to bear a daughter, bearing instead a son—the potential Kwisatz Haderach. She is a pivotal figure, imparting many Bene Gesserit skills to Paul and playing an immense role in his assimilation among the Fremen and his ascension as their leader (becoming also a Reverend Mother to them).

Development and Fate: Her path is one of constant conflict between duty to the Bene Gesserit, love for Leto and Paul, and her own volition. Following Leto's demise, she flees with Paul into the desert wastes, undergoes the Spice Agony, becomes the Reverend Mother of the Fremen, and aids Paul in his ascent to power.

Later, fearing the growing tyranny of the Muad'Dib cult and sensing danger for Alia, she returns to Caladan. In Children of Dune, she again intervenes in events, seeking to influence her grandchildren and to oppose

Alia, now overtaken by possession.

In the end, Jessica returns to the Sisterhood, remaining an influential figure throughout the later books (Heretics of Dune, Chapterhouse: Dune), where her genetic legacy and ancestral memory continue to shape events.

Core Traits: Strength of will, intellect, loyalty (conflicted), Bene Gesserit mastery (observation, control, the Voice), maternal devotion, dread of the future.

> *Voice (Quote)*: « *Fear is the mind-killer. Fear is the little-death that brings total obliteration. I will face my fear. I will permit it to pass over me and through me.* » *(The Litany Against Fear—her primary tool of self-mastery).*

3. Paul Atreides / Muad'Dib / Usul

Role and Significance: The central figure of the first novel and the protagonist of the initial trilogy.

Son of Duke Leto and Lady Jessica, heir to House Atreides, the culmination of generations of Bene Gesserit breeding, who becomes the Kwisatz Haderach and the messianic Mahdi of the Fremen. His rise and reign reshape the fate of the Imperium.

Development and Fate: Paul's arc is both epic and tragic.

He begins as a young noble trained in warcraft, politics, and Bene Gesserit disciplines and is then thrust into the crucible of the desert. As Muad'Dib, he leads the Fremen, gains absolute prescience through the Spice, defeats the Harkonnens and the Emperor, and ascends as the new Padishah Emperor.

Yet his victory unleashes a devastating Jihad across the galaxy—one he is powerless to halt, caught in the snare of his own prophetic vision.

In Dune Messiah, Paul confronts conspiracies, loses his physical sight to a stone burner attack, yet continues to "see" through prescience.

Ultimately, in order to avoid deification and the horrors of the future he foresees, he abdicates the throne and walks blind into the desert, following ancient Fremen custom.

He later reappears in Children of Dune as The Preacher—a blind prophet denouncing the cult of Muad'Dib and Alia's theocracy—only to be slain by her priests.

His legacy, both genetic and philosophical, remains central to the saga that follows.

Core Traits: Intellect, Bene Gesserit conditioning, charisma, a profound sense of duty, the burden of prescience, tragic stature—bound by the inability to alter a terrible future. Leadership, unwavering determination, and later in life—weariness and disillusionment.

> *Voice (Quote)*: « *Prophecy and prescience... how they trap you in a cage of inevitability.* » *(Reflecting on the nature of his gift.)*

4. Alia Atreides / St. Alia of the Knife

Role and Significance: Paul's younger sister, daughter of Duke Leto and Lady Jessica. Born after Jessica became a Reverend Mother, Alia acquired ancestral memory in utero—a Pre-born.

As a child, she possessed the consciousness and knowledge of a fully awakened Reverend Mother, which unsettled many around her.

She played a pivotal role in the final battle for Arrakeen, slaying Baron Vladimir Harkonnen. Later, she served as Regent of the Imperium during the minority of Paul's children.

Development and Fate: Alia's arc is one of the darkest tragedies in the saga.

As a Pre-born, she lacked a fully formed personal identity capable of withstanding the onslaught of ancestral voices in her genetic memory.

In Children of Dune, she becomes possessed by the consciousness of her grandfather—the Baron—and gradually descends into tyranny.

According to Bene Gesserit terminology, she becomes an Abomination, one whose soul has been overwhelmed by ancestral presences.

Her rule is marked by brutality and paranoia. As Leto II begins his transformation, Alia, unable to resist the Baron's influence, takes her own life.

Her tragedy stems not from her cruelty, but from the overwhelming burden of a gift that was too immense for a human child to bear.

Core Traits: Preternatural abilities from birth, isolation, the burden of being Pre-born, intellect, cruelty (later), possession, tragic downfall.

> *Voice (Quote)*: « My brother is a holy fool! » (Children of Dune — expressing her contempt for Paul and his legacy under the Baron's influence.)

5. Leto II Atreides / God Emperor

Role and Significance: Son of Paul Muad'Dib and Chani, twin brother of Ghanima. Also a Pre-born. Protagonist of Children of Dune and the central figure of the saga beyond Paul—particularly in God Emperor of Dune.

To save humanity from stagnation and eventual extinction—futures foreseen by his father—he chooses the Golden Path, a course of long tyranny and forced evolution.

Development and Fate: In Children of Dune, Leto embraces the choice Paul could not: he merges with sandtrout, initiating his transformation into a hybrid of human and sandworm, gaining near-immortality and heightened prescience.

He overthrows Alia and becomes the new Emperor.

In God Emperor of Dune, we encounter him 3,500 years later—transformed into a massive sandworm with a human face, yet still conscious as Leto II.

His reign—known as the Peace of Leto—halts wars and technological advancement, but forcibly scatters humanity across the galaxy (the Great Scattering).

He bred into humanity a gene—through the Atreides line of Siona—that rendered individuals invisible to prescience, ensuring that no prophet could ever again imprison the species within a single vision.

His rule ends with his own orchestrated assassination. He foresees his death and accepts it. His body dissolves, giving rise to new sandworms and restoring the Spice Cycle to the galaxy. His legacy—the Golden Path—shapes the fate of humanity for millennia to come.

Core Traits: Superhuman intellect and prescience, immense willpower, self-sacrifice (abandonment of humanity for a higher goal), loneliness (across 3,500 years), wisdom, calculated cruelty, paradoxical nature—a tyrant who saves.

> *Voice (Quote)*: « *The Golden Path is survival. Nothing else mattered.* » *(Explaining the essence of his reign.)*

6. Ghanima Atreides

Role and Significance: Daughter of Paul and Chani, twin sister to Leto II. Like her brother, she is Pre-born—possessing ancestral memory from the womb. She shares with Leto the early stages of the Golden Path and carries the genetic and spiritual legacy of House Atreides.

Development and Fate: In Children of Dune, Ghanima plays a crucial role as Leto's ally in the struggle against Alia.

To shield her consciousness from ancestral possession, she employs self-hypnosis, blocking dangerous memories and implanting a false one—convincing herself that Leto is dead.

Unlike her brother, she remains fully human.

She agrees to a political marriage with Farad'n Corrino, the last scion of House Corrino, in order to solidify Leto's power and continue the Atreides line.

In God Emperor of Dune, she is mentioned only as part of Leto II's genetic and ancestral memory. Her individual fate after Children of Dune is not detailed, though it is implied that she fulfilled her dynastic purpose.

Core Traits: Loyalty to her brother, strength of will, cunning, pragmatism, retention of humanity (in contrast to Leto II), the burden of being Pre-born.

Voice (Quote): « *Leto and I are one being in two bodies—you know that.* » *(Spoken of her bond with her brother in Children of Dune.)*

These are the central figures of House Atreides, whose lives form the spine of Frank Herbert's original saga. We now turn to other key figures drawn into the orbit of House Atreides.

Chapter 12: The Loyal of House Atreides

House Atreides was not only famed for its nobility but also for the exceptional devotion of those who served it. Duke Leto's innermost circle comprised distinguished specialists who became teachers, mentors, and companions to the young Paul. Their fates are inextricably linked with the rise and fall of the House.

1. Duncan Idaho

Role and Significance: The legendary Swordmaster of Ginaz, one of Duke Leto's most trusted and formidable warriors. A master of the blade and a loyal friend of the Atreides household. Duncan was the first Atreides envoy to the Fremen and earned their respect.

What makes Duncan unique is his persistence through time: resurrected as a series of gholas by the Bene Tleilax, he spans the entire saga of Frank Herbert, serving multiple generations of the Atreides—and more. He becomes the living thread that binds millennia of Dune's history.

Development and Fate: The original Duncan dies heroically on Arrakis, covering Paul and Jessica's escape from the Sardaukar.

The Tleilaxu preserve his cells and begin "resurrecting" him as gholas. The first ghola, Hayt, appears in Dune Messiah—a gift to Emperor Paul, secretly programmed to assassinate him. Hayt struggles with his implanted nature, falls in love with Alia, and in a moment of crisis, regains the memories and identity of the original Duncan.

In the following novels, Duncan's gholas serve—and at times rebel against—God Emperor Leto II for over 3,500 years. Leto values the "spark" of unpredictability and loyalty in them that he himself has lost.

After Leto's death, in Heretics of Dune and Chapterhouse: Dune, a new Duncan ghola is raised by the Bene Gesserit and becomes central to their struggle against the Honored Matres. He awakens hidden Tleilaxu abilities, and by the end of the sixth book, he departs aboard a no-ship with Sheeana and others into the uncharted reaches of the universe—carrying within him the memories of all previous iterations.

His repeated lives, deaths, and resurrections explore the themes of loyalty, identity, love, and the burden of memory.

Core Traits: Unsurpassed fidelity (particularly to the Atreides, creating conflicts for the gholas), martial mastery, charisma, impulsiveness, honesty, skepticism (initially), immense cumulative experience (as a ghola), complex romantic entanglements.

Voice (Quote - Ghola Hayt): « Loyalty to the ruling House demands that one sometimes act against orders. »

2. Gurney Halleck

Role and Significance: Weapons Master of House Atreides, warrior-bard, responsible for military training and security. One of Duke Leto's closest companions and among Paul's most important mentors.

Renowned for his virtuosity on the baliset and the inkvine scar etched across his jaw—a cruel gift from the Harkonnens, whom he hates not only for their torture but the murder of his family.

Development and Fate: In Dune, Gurney is the embodiment of House Atreides—sword, scar, and song in a single man.

He survives the downfall of the Atreides regime on Arrakis and joins a band of spice smugglers.

Later, he reunites with Paul and Jessica and becomes one of the key military leaders in the Fremen uprising.

His suspicion of Jessica—fueled by rumors planted by the Harkonnens—leads to a tense confrontation in which her loyalty is tested. His trust in her is then fully restored.

In Children of Dune, he remains an influential figure at the court of the regent Alia, maintaining fidelity to the Atreides legacy and aiding Jessica in her machinations against her possessed daughter. His fate following Leto II's ascension is not chronicled, but he endures as a symbol of the old Atreides guard.

Core Traits: Absolute loyalty, martial prowess, musical talent, forthrightness, gruff humor, scars of the past (physical and spiritual), consuming hatred for the Harkonnens.

Voice (Quote): « *Mood is for cattle and loveplay—not fighting.* »

3. Thufir Hawat

Role and Significance: Legendary Mentat-Assassin who served House Atreides across three generations. Master of strategy, logic, suspicion, and counterintelligence. Head of Duke Leto's security apparatus and tutor to Paul. Considered the greatest Mentat of his time.

Development and Fate: His story is the tragedy of a great mind brought low by a fatal error.

Despite his deep-seated suspicion and analytical brilliance, he failed to detect the traitor in Dr. Yueh—an oversight that led directly to the fall of House Atreides. That failure becomes his personal torment.

Captured by the Harkonnens, he is coerced into serving Baron Vladimir under the threat of a slow, painful death by poison—the antidote granted only in measured doses.

Hawat attempts simultaneously to serve his new masters, sabotage their designs, and exact vengeance upon the supposed culprits behind the fall of the Atreides (the Emperor and—as he erroneously believed—Lady Jessica).

In the climax of Dune, the Emperor commands him to kill Paul. Instead, Hawat finds a way to reclaim his loyalty to his final Atreides duke—and dies by activating the poison in his body. A Mentat to the end.

Core Traits: Genius-level intellect, impeccable logic, loyalty (driven to self-destruction), pervasive suspicion, mastery of intrigue, burden of guilt, stoicism.

Voice (Quote): « *Logic is merely a tool. Purpose dictates its application.* » *(A reflection of Mentat pragmatism.)*

4. Dr. Wellington Yueh

Role and Significance: Personal physician to House Atreides and a graduate of the prestigious Suk School. His Imperial Conditioning—symbolized by the black diamond tattoo on his forehead—was designed to ensure absolute loyalty and nonviolence toward those under his care. That's why his betrayal was so devastating... and so unexpected.

Development and Fate: A tragic figure, broken by the Harkonnens. The Baron captured and tortured Yueh's beloved wife, Wanna, offering her life in exchange for Yueh's betrayal of Duke Leto. Desperation and false hope drove him to agree. He deactivated the palace shields at Arrakeen and enabled the enemy's infiltration. Yet he retained a fragment of loyalty. He arranged for Paul and Jessica to escape and gave Leto a poisoned tooth in a final attempt to kill the Baron—an attempt that failed.

Immediately after fulfilling his end of the bargain, Yueh was executed by Piter de Vries at the Baron's command. Wanna had been dead all along.

His story is a grim reminder that no conditioning is absolute—and even the most seemingly unbreakable codes can be undone by love, grief, and human frailty.

Core Traits: Medical excellence, hidden sorrow, despair, guilt, coerced betrayal, tragic figure.

> **Voice (Quote)**: « *There is no beast more savage than a man deprived of love.* » (*A phrase essentially explaining his motivation*).

They came from Caladan, bearing honor and loyalty. Their likenesses endured upon the sands of Arrakis—not as mere shadows of the past but as voices to whom Paul would turn time and again, even as he himself ascended to godhood and legend.

But Paul's story is not just memory and loss. His path would be impossible without those who lived—and died—in the desert.

Next come the Fremen.

Chapter 13: The Fremen: Children of Dune

The desert folk, descendants of the Zensunni Wanderers—the Fremen, or the Free—embody the ultimate human adaptation to the harshest of environments.

Their culture is built upon ruthless water discipline, communal solidarity (the tribe is one family), martial prowess, and a deep, almost mystical connection to the desert, to the Spice, and to Shai-Hulud. Once ignored or scorned by the Imperium, they would become the force that reshaped the galaxy.

1. Stilgar

Role and Significance: A powerful and wise Naib (chieftain) of Sietch Tabr, one of the largest and most influential Fremen communities. Stilgar becomes a key figure in welcoming Paul and Jessica, serving as Paul's mentor in the ways of the desert and Fremen custom—and later, as one of his most loyal generals and trusted friends.

He is the embodiment of traditional Fremen values: pragmatism, honor, loyalty to tribe, and profound reverence for the desert.

Development and Fate: In Dune, Stilgar evolves from a cautious leader suspicious of outsiders into a devoted follower of Muad'Dib, recognizing in him the fulfillment of ancient prophecy. He plays a crucial role in training Paul and integrating him into Fremen society.

After Paul's victory, Stilgar remains a prominent figure at the new imperial court. But in Dune Messiah—and more deeply in Children of Dune—his character is explored with greater complexity: he struggles with the cultural upheavals brought by the Atreides rule—terraforming, the erosion of tradition, the bureaucratization of Fremen life, and the devastating consequences of the Jihad.

He is torn between his fierce loyalty to Paul and his children (Leto II and Ghanima), and his sorrow over the loss of the old Fremen way.

He remains faithful to the last, shielding Paul's children from Alia's machinations. His figure symbolizes the tragedy of an old world yielding to the new, even if this new world was the objective of their struggle.

Core Traits: Desert wisdom, strength, leadership, pragmatism, deep faith and traditionalism, unwavering loyalty (at times blind), a sense of responsibility, and honor.

> **Voice (Quote)**: « We must change... They say water is life. We forget—it is also death. » (Stilgar, reflecting on terraforming in Children of Dune).

2. Chani

Role and Significance: Daughter of planetologist Liet-Kynes and his Fremen wife, Chani is a fierce warrior and a Sayyadina (acolyte of the Reverend Mother) within her tribe. She becomes Paul Muad'Dib's beloved—his concubine under Imperial law but his only true wife by Fremen custom and by the law of the heart.

She is the mother of his twin children, Leto II and Ghanima. To Paul, she is not only a lover but his living bond to Arrakis, to the desert people—his sihaya, the spring of the desert.

Development and Fate: Chani manifests in Paul's earliest prescient visions even before his arrival upon Arrakis. Their meeting and subsequent love form a central element of his transformation into Muad'Dib.

She stands by him through every trial—through life in the sietch, in battle, and in love.

She endures Paul's political marriage to Irulan with strength, knowing that by soul and blood he belongs to her.

In Dune Messiah, her pregnancy becomes the target of a conspiracy—Irulan, under the influence of Paul's enemies, secretly administers contraceptives to her. Despite this, Chani eventually carries their children.

She dies tragically in childbirth, and her loss devastates Paul—driving him toward his final withdrawal into the desert. Her image remains sacred to her children and the entire Cult of Muad'Dib. Later, the Bene Tleilaxu craft her ghola, attempting to manipulate Duncan Idaho, but her legacy proves stronger than their plans.

Core Traits: Strength of spirit, independence, warrior's ferocity, profound love for and devotion to Paul, Fremen endurance and pragmatism, understanding of the desert, motherhood.

> *Voice (Quote)*: « *Tell me of the waters of your homeworld, Usul.* » *(A simple yet significant phrase, revealing her interest in Paul, their intimacy, and the contrast between their worlds).*

3. Liet-Kynes

Role and Significance: A singular figure who bridges two worlds. Officially, he is the Imperial Planetologist of Arrakis—a scientist appointed by the Emperor to study the planet.

In secret, however, he is the son of the previous planetologist, Pardot Kynes, and a Fremen woman. Following his father's death, he becomes the hidden leader of the Fremen, who revere him as a prophet. ("Liet"—in the Fremen tongue—means "community" or "gathering.") He bears the legacy of his father's dream: to transform Dune into a flourishing green world.

Development and Fate: In Dune, Liet appears as a respected expert assisting House Atreides—yet he remains aloof, his loyalty bound to clandestine goals.

He sees in Paul Atreides a possible key to realizing his ecological dream of reshaping the planet.

After the fall of House Atreides, Liet breaks his neutrality and helps Paul and Jessica escape into the desert. For this, he is captured by the Harkonnens and left to die—alone, without a stillsuit, in the merciless sands.

As he succumbs, under the influence of the pre-spice mass, he experiences visions of his father and attains a final, searing clarity—grasping both the greatness and the peril of transforming Arrakis.

Core Traits: Dual nature (scientist and hidden leader), deep ecological knowledge, pragmatism, secrecy, idealism (the dream of terraforming), scientific mind, devotion to the people of the desert.

> *Voice (Quote):* « *Beyond the cities, we are all Fremen.* » *(A key phrase that reveals where his true loyalties lie).*

These three are the heart of the desert—the essence of the Fremen spirit. They helped shape Paul into Muad'Dib yet remained true to themselves: sons and daughters of Dune.

Now, let us turn to those who lurk in the industrial depths of their homeworld, where the sun is naught but a dim mirage glimpsed through a veil of smoke. To those whose name became synonymous with fear:

House Harkonnen.

Chapter 14: House Harkonnen: The Path of Fear and Deceit

If the Atreides symbolize honor and justice, their sworn enemies—the Harkonnens—embody tyranny, greed, and unrelenting treachery.

Their path is one of manipulation, cruelty, and an insatiable pursuit of power, unchecked by any moral restraint.

1. Baron Vladimir Harkonnen

Role and Significance: The magnetic and monstrous heart of House Harkonnen, Siridar of Giedi Prime. A master of shadowplay and systemic cruelty, Baron Vladimir Harkonnen stands as the central antagonist to Duke Leto and Paul Atreides in Dune—a symbol of everything the Atreides are not. He is a tyrant cloaked in opulence, a strategist whose mind is as sharp as his morals are absent.

His grotesque corpulence—so immense that he must float on suspensors like some obscene parody of gravitas—is rumored to be the result of either a degenerative disease or a genetic reprisal by the Bene Gesserit. But regardless of its origin, it lays bare the essence of his being: a man who devours—food, power, and people—with the same bottomless hunger. To him, cruelty is not indulgence—it is efficiency. Mercy is waste.

Development and Fate: The Baron is the great manipulator, weaving plans within plans, ensnaring the Emperor, traitors within House Atreides, and even his own nephew, Feyd-Rautha, in a web devised to annihilate the Atreides and reclaim dominion over Arrakis and its Spice.

His scheme comes perilously close to fruition—but he underestimates the desert, the weight of prophecy, and the depth of Fremen loyalty. Though he survives Duke Leto's assassination attempt via poison tooth (which claims the life of his Mentat, Piter de Vries), his end comes by blood, not blade or bomb.

At the height of the Fremen assault on Arrakeen, he is assassinated by his own granddaughter—Alia Atreides, daughter of Jessica, whose Harkonnen bloodline he never knew. She is both his kin and his reckoning, and she slays him with a gom jabbar—the very weapon used to test whether one is human.

Yet even in death, the Baron is not finished. In Children of Dune, his ancestral presence—lodged within Alia's Other Memory—rises again, corrupting her from within and turning her into an Abomination. Through her, his malevolent will persists, a foul echo of tyranny refusing to fade.

Core Traits: Genius for perfidy, absolute amorality, sadism, insatiable greed and appetites (in every sense), mastery of manipulation, paranoia, depravity, acute intellect.

Voice (Quote): « *Observe the plans within plans within plans,* » *the Baron once told Feyd-Rautha. The phrase, deceptively simple, reflects the very architecture of the Imperium—where loyalty, power, and truth are layered like traps, each concealing another beneath it.*

2. Feyd-Rautha Harkonnen

Role and Significance: The younger nephew and favored heir of Baron Vladimir Harkonnen—his chosen na-Baron. In every way the antithesis of his brutish cousin, Glossu Rabban, Feyd is handsome, intelligent, and charismatic (by Harkonnen standards), a golden boy groomed for dominance. On the industrial nightmare of Giedi Prime, he is a celebrity—adored by the masses.

To the Baron, he represents the future of the House—and a pivotal piece in the Bene Gesserit's breeding program: a potential father to the Kwisatz Haderach, had he been paired with an Atreides daughter.

Development and Fate: The Baron grooms Feyd meticulously, cultivating his image through staged gladiatorial victories and training him in the arts of intrigue. But Feyd harbors ambitions of his own—plotting even to assassinate his uncle.

At the end of Dune, following the downfall of Emperor Shaddam IV, Feyd challenges Paul to a kanly duel, hoping to seize power. Despite his attempt to cheat using concealed poisoned blades, he is slain by Paul in single combat.

Core Traits: Ambition, cunning, cruelty masked by charm, athleticism, popularity, vanity, and genetic potential (in Bene Gesserit terms).

> **Voice (Quote)**: « *That woman you were speaking to—the small one. Is she special to you? A pet, perhaps? Shall I give her... special attention?* » *(Taunting Paul during their duel — Dune, 1965).*

3. Glossu "The Beast" Rabban

Role and Significance: The elder nephew of Baron Vladimir Harkonnen and brother to Feyd-Rautha. In every way Feyd's opposite—brutish, immensely strong, and mindlessly cruel.

Rabban is the Baron's blunt instrument: installed as governor of Arrakis after the fall of House Atreides, tasked with ruling through terror. The

Baron's strategy is as ruthless as it is calculated: break the population with Rabban's tyranny, then replace him with the "merciful" Feyd-Rautha—whom the people would embrace as a savior.

Development and Fate: The plan unfolds exactly as intended—until it doesn't. What was meant to break the spirit of the people only hardens it. Rabban's reign following the fall of House Atreides becomes infamous for its unchecked violence, greed, and incompetence, only fueling the Fremen resistance and deepening their support for Paul Muad'Dib. Unable to counter guerrilla warfare or grasp the depth of the Fremen threat, Rabban becomes a liability. He is ultimately killed during the Fremen assault on Arrakeen.

Core Traits: Unrestrained rage, blunt cruelty, immense physical strength, shortsightedness, greed, and a total lack of strategic insight.

> *Voice (Quote)*: *(His actions speak louder than words)* « *Crush them! More Spice! Make them pay!* »

4. Piter de Vries

Role and Significance: A twisted Mentat and sadistic genius in service to Baron Harkonnen. What sets Piter apart is his rare fusion of Mentat intellect, deviant cruelty, and a deep addiction to melange—an unusual trait among Mentats, who traditionally pursue clarity through untainted logic. He serves as the Baron's chief advisor, strategist, and 'mind' at the commencement of Dune.

Development and Fate: It is Piter who devises the intricate details of the plot to annihilate House Atreides, including the manipulation of Doctor Yueh. He is brilliant, cynical, and takes perverse delight in the suffering of others. Yet his addiction to Spice and his sadistic impulses makes him volatile and unpredictable.

He perishes in the Baron's stead—slain by Duke Leto's poison capsule tooth during the Duke's capture. His death deprives the Baron of his most vital intellectual asset.

Core Traits: Keen Mentat intellect, depravity, sadism, Spice addiction, cynicism, ruthless efficiency, fidelity to the Baron.

Voice (Quote - Baron Harkonnen about Piter): « *At times, I ponder Piter... I inflict pain as a necessity, but he... I vow, derives explicit pleasure therefrom.* »

Baron, Feyd, Rabban, Piter—each reveal that evil wears many masks: refined or brutish, calculated or unhinged. Their methods horrify. Their legacy corrupts everything it touches.

Yet above even their blackened wills loomed a greater force—crowned in imperial gold, cloaked in old fear: the House Corrino.

Chapter 15: The Imperial Throne: Radiance and Sunset of House Corrino

For ten millennia, House Corrino ruled the Known Universe from the Golden Lion Throne. But by the opening of Dune, their grip on power is no longer absolute. Intrigue and fear of rising rivals drive them toward dangerous decisions.

1. Padishah Emperor Shaddam IV Corrino

Role and Significance: The 81st Emperor of the Corrino dynasty, ruler of the Known Universe. The pivotal figure behind the conspiracy against House Atreides, though acting through the hands of others (namely, the Harkonnens). His fear of Duke Leto's waxing influence becomes the catalyst for the events of the first novel.

Development and Fate: Shaddam IV is portrayed as a cunning yet shortsighted and vain sovereign. He authorizes the destruction of House Atreides, lending the Harkonnens his elite Sardaukar. When Paul Muad'Dib sparks a rebellion on Arrakis and brings the Spice flow to a halt, Shaddam is forced to intervene personally.

He arrives on Dune at the head of a vast imperial fleet—only to suffer a crushing defeat at the hands of the sandworm-riding Fremen. In the denouement, Paul compels him to abdicate the throne and demands the hand of Princess Irulan to legitimize the new regime. Saddam is exiled to Salusa Secundus, and the thousand-year rule of House Corrino effectively comes to an end.

Core Traits: Ambition, cunning, paranoia, political instinct (clouded by fatal miscalculations), vanity, dependence on the Sardaukar.

Voice (Quote): « *Silence! You have no rights here!* » *(The bark of a ruler who senses the end—clutching at power already slipping through his fingers.)*

2. Princess Irulan Corrino

Role and Significance: The eldest of Shaddam IV's five daughters, trained by the Bene Gesserit. An intelligent, educated, and beautiful aristocrat. She becomes the official wife of Emperor Muad'Dib. Irulan is also notable as a chronicler—many chapters in the saga open with excerpts from her writings, offering the reader historical context and philosophical reflection.

Development and Fate: Initially a political pawn, Irulan is wed to Paul not out of love, but to forge a dynastic alliance. Paul remains devoted to Chani. In Dune Messiah, she participates in the conspiracy against Paul, secretly administering contraceptives to Chani to ensure Paul remains without legitimate heirs. Yet she does so not purely out of malice but from loyalty to her deposed father and perhaps from unrequited love and jealousy toward Paul.

She later repents, manifests respect for Paul and Chani, and becomes caretaker to his children, Leto II and Ghanima following Chani's death and Paul's departure into the desert. In Children of Dune, she remains loyal to House Atreides and chronicles the history of Muad'Dib. Her long life—sustained by Spice—and her writings make her one of the era's most important witnesses.

Core Traits: Intellect, erudition (Bene Gesserit trained), beauty, sense of duty, inner conflict, observational skill, historian's talent.

> *Voice (Quote)*: « *Muad'Dib could indeed see the Future, but you must understand the limits of this power...* » *(From 'Analysis: The Arrakis Crisis' by the Princess Irulan).*

3. Count Hasimir Fenring

Role and Significance: The closest (and perhaps only true) friend of Emperor Shaddam IV since childhood. Though technically head of a Minor House (see Chapter 4), Fenring was one of the most influential figures at court. A consummate spy, political assassin ("the Emperor's blade in the shadows"), and trusted confidant. A genetic eunuch and failed Kwisatz Haderach—a unique outcome of the Bene Gesserit breeding program, in which he participated indirectly through his wife, Lady Margot.

Development and Fate: Fenring functions as the éminence grise to Shaddam. He acts as his eyes and ears, assessing the Harkonnens and the Atreides. He possesses uncanny insight and an empathetic capacity, bordering upon the ability to read minds. In the denouement of Dune, when Shaddam commands him to assassinate Paul following Feyd-Rautha's defeat, Fenring, recognizing Paul's true power (perhaps owing to his link to the Bene Gesserit program or simply from pragmatism), refuses the command. This refusal marks the final humiliation of Shaddam IV. Fenring departs into exile alongside his Emperor.

Core Traits: Supreme intellect, cunning, penetrating insight, empathy, mastery of espionage, fidelity to the Emperor (near-absolute), stealth, genetic anomaly.

Voice (Quote): « *The boy lacks patience,* » *Fenring whispered.* « *And he makes mistakes when he's fascinated.* » *(Regarding Feyd-Rautha; revealing Fenring's keen observation).*

These three figures—Emperor, Princess, Confidant—embodied an imperial power whose age had reached its twilight. Accustomed to shaping destinies from behind silken draperies, they failed to notice how the desert dust had already seeped through the palace walls. And the galaxy, long obedient to their banner, was already stirring to the summons of another.

Chapter 16: The Bene Gesserit: Weavers of the Threads of Destiny

Within the shadows of the Imperium, weavers of destiny have always stirred. But none have shaped the course of history with such subtlety, persistence, and cold precision as the ancient Sisterhood of the Bene Gesserit (see Chapter 7). Through religion, selective breeding, and calculated alliances, they have steered humanity toward their own cryptic ends.

Let us now observe those who tugged at the finest threads.

1. Reverend Mother Gaius Helen Mohiam

Role and Significance: One of the most influential Reverend Mothers of her age, Truthsayer to Padishah Emperor Shaddam IV and former mentor to Lady Jessica. She served as the voice of the Sisterhood at court and the arbiter of Paul's destiny on the first day of his testing.

It is Mohiam who administers the Gom Jabbar ordeal to the young Atreides heir, seeking to uncover his true nature—and assess the threat he may pose to the centuries-old plan.

Development and Fate: Mohiam is the living embodiment of Bene Gesserit power and cold calculation. Her apprehension regarding Paul's birth (in place of their daughter Jessica had been commanded to bear) swiftly transmutes into dread of a Kwisatz Haderach beyond the Sisterhood's control.

Following Paul's ascension, she becomes party to the great conspiracy against Muad'Dib. Blackmail, covert pacts with the Tleilaxu and the Spacing Guild—all in the name of preserving the established balance. But the universe had shifted, and the ancient stratagems no longer availed.

Mohiam perishes—slain by Stilgar as he defends Paul's children. Her death marks the collapse of the old powers' final attempt to contain the phenomenon that was Muad'Dib.

Core Traits: Commanding presence, piercing insight (as a Truthsayer), ruthlessness, unwavering loyalty to the Bene Gesserit Order, political cunning, conservatism, and fear of powers beyond control.

> *Voice (Quote):* « *The test is simple: remove your hand from the box and you die.* » *(During Paul's Gom Jabbar test).*

2. Lady Margot Fenring

Role and Significance: Clad in silk and grace—with every word echoing the veiled commands of the Sisterhood. Elegant and astute, Lady Margot Fenring is the wife of Count Hasimir Fenring, yet her true loyalty lies neither with her husband nor with the Emperor—but with the Bene Gesserit. Dispatched to Giedi Prime as an agent of the highest caliber, tasked with a specific mission.

Development and Fate: Her task in Dune is to assess Feyd-Rautha Harkonnen as a potential link in the breeding program and—more crucially—to secure his genetic contribution by conceiving a child, thereby preserving the Harkonnen line outside a direct Atreides-Harkonnen union. She executes this task with cold precision: for her, charm honed to automatism and the art of seduction are instruments of duty, not passion.

Additionally, she leaves behind a covert warning for Lady Jessica—a gesture that may arise from sisterly solidarity, or perhaps strict adherence to deeper instructions.

Following the fall of Shaddam IV, Margot departs into exile alongside her husband. The ultimate fate of her child by Feyd remains unwritten in canon.

Core Traits: Intellect, charm, cunning, Bene Gesserit discipline, adeptness at seduction and manipulation, keen observation, devotion to the Order.

> *Voice (Quote):* « *I dreamed about you last night.* » *(Uttered during her calculated seduction of Feyd-Rautha)*

3. Mother Superior Taraza

Role and Significance: Reverend Mother Taraza stands as the head of the Bene Gesserit during the events of Heretics of Dune and Chapterhouse: Dune—nearly five thousand years after the era of Muad'Dib. Her leadership arises at a time of existential crisis: the return of the Honored Matres from the Scattering—an overwhelming, violent force that threatens to unravel both the Imperium and the Sisterhood itself. Taraza emerged as the voice of reason in an age when ancient dogmas no longer sufficed.

Development and Fate: She weaves a delicate yet brilliant stratagem of resistance—through the Duncan Idaho ghola, Bashar Miles Teg, and through the very nature of the relationship with the Honored Matres. Taraza sought prophecies, not weaknesses —and founded her stratagems upon the enemy's fears. She knowingly goes to her death in a confrontation with the Great Honored Matre on Rakis (formerly Arrakis), having first transferred the entirety of Other Memory to her successor, Darwi Odrade. Thus, her plan lives on even beyond her own demise.

Core Traits: Foresight, strategic genius, profound psychological insight, pragmatism, willingness for self-sacrifice, fidelity to the Order, skill in manipulating the future through fear, not prescience.

> *Voice (Quote):* «We cannot afford the luxury of moral absolutes if we wish to survive.» (Reflecting Bene Gesserit pragmatism when facing existential threat).

4. Mother Superior Darwi Odrade

Role and Significance: A Reverend Mother of Atreides descent—descended from Siona, whose genes render her invisible to prescience. She ascends as the successor to Taraza and becomes Mother Superior of the Bene Gesserit at the height of their war with the Honored Matres. Odrade stands as the central figure of Frank Herbert's final novel, Chapterhouse: Dune.

Development and Fate: Odrade is compelled to lead the Order through the darkest hour of its history. She blends traditional Bene Gesserit wisdom with a distinct measure of the Atreides sense of honor and even compassion. She seeks to comprehend the nature of the Honored Matres, while continuing to utilize the Duncan and Teg gholas. Odrade directs the terraforming of the planet Chapterhouse into a new Dune for the rebirth of the sandworms and independence from the old sources of the Spice.

In the novel's climax, she perishes in a confrontation with the Honored Matres but succeeds in transferring her Other Memory to Murbella (a captured Matre who embraces the Bene Gesserit path) and to Sheeana, thus preserving the collective wisdom—and perhaps the very survival—of the Sisterhood in a transformed future.

Core Traits: Wisdom, compassion, pragmatism, strategic acumen, profound connection to her Atreides heritage, leadership, courage, curiosity.

> **Voice (Quote)**: « *Survival is the ability to swim in strange water.* » *(Reflecting Bene Gesserit adaptability in the face of new dangers).*

These figures reveal the Bene Gesserit to be more than merely a secret Order. They embody memory spanning millennia. At times allies, at times antagonists, yet always—guardians of human potential, as they perceive it.

Chapter 17: Other Key Figures of the Saga

The legacy of the early generations shapes the fate of those who follow. These subsequent figures play pivotal roles in the unfolding themes and plotlines of Frank Herbert's original six-book saga—heirs, instruments, or adversaries of the grand designs forged previously.

1. Bashar Miles Teg

Role and Significance: Legendary Supreme Bashar (highest military rank) of the Bene Gesserit order, a living legend of the Imperium, renowned for his tactical genius and unswerving fidelity to the Sisterhood. A descendant of House Atreides, a lineage manifested in his appearance and sense of honor. Father of Reverend Mother Darwi Odrade. His recall from retirement becomes a pivotal event in the Bene Gesserit's confrontation with the Honored Matres.

Development and Fate: In Heretics of Dune, the aged Bashar is summoned to protect and train the latest Duncan Idaho ghola. He becomes embroiled in the war with the Honored Matres. Captured and subjected to torture using the forbidden T-Probe, he experiences a traumatic awakening of latent atavistic abilities: his body and mind accelerate to superhuman speeds, enabling him to move faster than sight can follow and to calculate tactics with preternatural efficiency. He orchestrates a daring escape and inflicts a devastating blow upon the Honored Matre forces on the planet Gammu yet perishes himself amidst the ensuing chaos.

In Chapterhouse: Dune, the Bene Gesserit, working with the Tleilaxu, commission the creation of his ghola. This new Teg, gradually recovering his memories and once again possessing his extraordinary abilities, becomes the Sisterhood's crucial military asset in the final conflict. Together with Duncan and Shiana, he departs into the unknown aboard a no-ship.

Core Traits: Military genius, tactical acumen, absolute fidelity to the Bene Gesserit, Atreides sense of honor, fortitude, latent superhuman abilities (accelerated reflexes/cognition), mentor figure.

Voice (Quote): « *Fear is a bad general. But an excellent scout.* »

2. Moneo Atreides

Role and Significance: Chief aide, majordomo, and—perhaps—the God Emperor Leto II's only true confidant during the long arc of his 3,500-year reign. The latest in a long line of Atreides descendants (likely through Ghanima), Moneo serves as our eyes and ears within the court of the Worm. He is a man striving to serve and comprehend a nearly divine tyrant. Father of Siona.

Development and Fate: In God Emperor of Dune, Moneo presents as a faithful, yet profoundly weary servant. He executes Leto II's commands, manages the Fish Speakers, yet constantly experiences fear and existential dread before his Lord and the Golden Path. He attempts to shield his daughter Siona—both from her own rebellion and from the God Emperor's designs.

In the novel's climax, Moneo perishes alongside Leto II during the assassination orchestrated by Siona and the current Duncan Idaho ghola. The bridge upon which they stand collapses into the turbulent Idaho River—so named in Duncan's honor. This scene marks the culmination of the complex, near-sacred bond between Moneo and his Lord. Perishing beside the God Emperor whom he served all his life—and unto the end—becomes the ultimate act of tragic fidelity and the final punctuation of his path.

Core Traits: Dutifulness, loyalty (bordering on fear and adoration), administrative competence, internal struggle (faith vs. doubt), weariness from eternity (another's), paternal love.

3. Siona Atreides

Role and Significance: Daughter of Moneo, a distant descendant of the Atreides line. Leader of the underground resistance against the God Emperor. Yet her most critical role is not political but genetic: Siona is the living embodiment of the Golden Path's ultimate goal. As a result of Leto II's millennia-spanning breeding program, she—and her descendants—possess a unique genetic trait: they are completely invisible to all forms of prescience. Neither the God Emperor nor the Navigators of the Spacing Guild can perceive her future. She represents the antidote to prophetic tyranny and the key to ensuring that no seer can ever again imprison humanity within a single, inevitable vision.

Development and Fate: In God Emperor of Dune, Siona emerges as a fierce and impassioned rebel, driven by hatred of the Worm and the rigid world he has created. Leto II subjects her to a harrowing ordeal—the Trial of Siona—forcing her to witness firsthand the existential threats facing humanity and the necessity of the Golden Path. She survives the trial but remains an implacable opponent of Leto II. Together with the current Duncan Idaho ghola, she orchestrates the assassination that leads to the God Emperor's death.

Although Leto could not foresee the specific details of his demise—Siona's prescience-immunity shielding her from all prophetic vision—he anticipated that such a death would come. He understood that someone like her must exist, someone outside his control. Her survival and the future dissemination of her gene were the final, essential steps of his plan. Thus, her role in his death was not a failure of his foresight but the culmination of his vision. Siona, and her eventual union with Duncan, give rise to a new chapter in humanity's evolution—one liberated from the shackles of determinism.

Core Traits: Rebellious spirit, hatred of tyranny and stagnation, courage, Atreides fortitude, genetic singularity (invisibility to prescience), pivotal figure of the Golden Path.

> *Voice (Quote)*: « Siona is a woman of action. She lives on the surface of enormous energies which fill me with fantasies of delight. » (Leto II's observation on Siona's nature and vitality).

4. Sheeana Brugh

Role and Significance: An orphan discovered upon Rakis, possessing the unique, seemingly innate ability to command the great sandworms. Her existence immediately attracts the Bene Gesserit's profound interest, marking her as a figure of immense potential significance—perhaps representing a future pathway for humanity's relationship with the desert power, independent of Sisterhood manipulation.

Development and Fate: Brought into the Bene Gesserit fold following the devastation of Rakis, Sheeana undergoes their rigorous training upon Chapterhouse. She forms complex bonds with the Duncan Idaho and Miles Teg gholas, becoming integral to the Sisterhood's desperate stratagems. Alongside Murbella, she is a recipient of Darwi Odrade's final Other Memory transference before escaping the siege of Chapterhouse aboard the no-ship, venturing into an unknown future beyond the grasp of prophecy or pursuit.

Core Traits: Unique communion with sandworms, profound resilience, adaptability, enigmatic origins, latent power, Bene Gesserit conditioning.

5. Murbella

Role and Significance: An Honored Matre taken captive, initially embodying the ferocious, sexually dominating power of the returning forces from the Scattering. Her enforced capture and transformation position her as a volatile, potential bridge—or battleground—between the Bene Gesserit Sisterhood and its seemingly antithetical counterpart. Her bond with the Duncan Idaho ghola proves central to this dangerous synthesis.

Development and Fate: Imprisoned upon Chapterhouse, Murbella is subjected to the Spice Agony under duress. She survives the ordeal, integrating the Bene Gesserit's collective Other Memory (including Darwi Odrade's) with her innate Honored Matre abilities and worldview—a unique and perilous fusion. Ultimately joining the desperate flight aboard the no-ship, her escape embodies the uncertain hope for humanity's future path, one born from the violent merging of conflicting legacies.

Core Traits: Honored Matre combat prowess and sexual imprinting, Radical Adaptability, Integrated Other Memory, Volatile Leadership Potential, Fierce Independence.

Through the fates of Teg, Moneo, Siona, Sheeana, and Murbella sound the complex and final chords of the Golden Path and the era after it. Sacrifice, fear, rebellion, adaptation, and hope for an unknown future—in these figures was reflected the price of the great plan and the first steps beyond its bounds.

In Herbert's vision, humanity's true evolution lies not in machines, but in the burden of choice. And even a choice made millennia ago may demand payment only now.

Chapter 18: Deep Currents — Thematic and Philosophical Foundations of Dune

Though the intrigues, prophecies, and destinies of the Great Houses captivate from the first pages, the universe of Dune offers the reader something far more profound. It stands as a philosophical experiment in which every idea is tested through action, and every force is measured by its ability to endure. Frank Herbert employs science fiction not as escapism, but as a lens to reveal how subtle yet powerful forces—ranging from ecology to religion—shape not only civilizations, but the essence of what it means to be human. Here, there are no simple answers—only complex interdependencies. It is through these themes that the true depth of Dune is revealed.

Ecology as Destiny: The Interaction of Humanity and Environment

« *The highest function of ecology is the understanding of consequences.* » — *Frank Herbert*

Arrakis is not merely a planet—it is a thought experiment where nature itself becomes judge, teacher, and God. Ecology in Dune is not a backdrop to the plot but a driving force of civilization. Herbert demonstrates that environment shapes behavior, thought, and systems of power. Those who ignore the ecosystem are doomed. Those who align with it survive—and evolve.

The Fremen are not merely survivors—they are a people shaped and tested by the Desert. Every aspect of their culture—technology, faith, language—emerges from the unforgiving demands of life on Arrakis. The stillsuit is not a garment but a philosophy embodied in fabric: not worn for display but for survival. Their reverence for water is not ritualistic; it is ecological. In a world where a drop can mean life or death, even tears are a sacred act.

Politics, too, is subordinate to ecology. The Spice—the lifeblood of the Imperium—is not artificially produced. It is born within the life cycle of the sandworm, which itself depends on the desert. This creates an economy utterly dependent on a single natural process—and, therefore, inherently vulnerable to it. Destroy Arrakis, and you destroy the Spice. Destroy the Spice, and the Imperium crumbles. Thus, Herbert elevates nature to the level of imperial power, mightier than any fleet or legion.

Herbert underscores: any technological, political, or military system devised in ignorance of its ecosystem is destined, sooner or later, to collapse. Humankind does not control nature—it is woven into its fabric. In this sense, Arrakis is not a hostile planet but a harsh arbiter. And only by enduring its trial may one attain not dominion—but comprehension.

Thus, ecology in Dune concerns itself less with 'protecting nature' in the contemporary sense, and more with comprehending the long-term consequences of all actions and perceiving intricate interdependencies where others perceive only resources for exploitation or obstacles for surmounting. Herein lies one of Frank Herbert's principal ecological prophecies.

> A Question for Reflection: Am I a part of my environment—or do I still imagine myself separate from it?

The Game of Thrones of the Galaxy

> *« Power attracts the corruptible. Suspect all who seek it. »* — Frank Herbert

Politics in Dune is not a mere shuffle of rulers and banners. It is a meticulously layered hierarchy where power is inherited, upheld by economics, and enforced through fear and mutual dependence. Herbert does not simply imagine a feudalism of the future—he lays bare its inner mechanics: stability through violence, tradition, and manipulation.

The Imperium is a structure devoid of democracy yet steeped in stability. The Great Houses, the Landsraad, the Emperor, and the Spacing Guild are bound together by pacts and reciprocal coercion. No single power may defeat them all, but any can destroy another. This delicate equilibrium is what sustains the system. Herbert constructs here a political "nuclear deterrence."

CHOAM governs the economy, the Guild controls transportation, the Bene Gesserit wield ideological power. None of these factions dismantles the Imperium—instead, each act as a safeguard against absolute control. In this design, there is no total dominion—only fleeting supremacy.

Paul Atreides breaks this order. He does not enter the game as a player but a messianic force. His triumph over the Harkonnens and the Emperor is not merely a military conquest—it is the collapse of the entire balance of power. Paul's authority is not legitimized—it is sanctified by prophecy. This shatters the feudal structure and ignites the Jihad.

Yet Herbert does not glorify revolution. He reveals that replacing one system with another, absent understanding of power's architecture, leads only to catastrophe. The Jihad of Muad'Dib is not liberation—it is a new incarnation of fear.

The true mastery of politics in Dune lies in preserving equilibrium not in conquest:

+ *The Harkonnens need not be destroyed* — they can be weakened through leverage involving the Guild, as Leto contemplates on Caladan in the early chapters: he not only discusses the military threat with Thufir Hawat but the possibility of using economic influence and Guild connections to escape the snare set by the Emperor and the Harkonnens. He does not seek open confrontation but rather a way to navigate the system's logic and bend it to his will.

✦ *Resistance need not be crushed* — it can be channeled. Leto II, in God Emperor of Dune, never entirely suppresses rebellion; instead, he allows it to persist in controlled forms, preserving dominance through the illusion of choice.

✦ *Even wielding absolute power, Leto II weaves opposition into the fabric of Empire*: he lets the Atreides bloodline endure and permits both the Guild and the Bene Tleilaxu a measure of autonomy. This is not weakness—it is the art of transforming threat into structure.

Not every threat requires elimination—sometimes it serves as a pillar of balance. Through the political architecture of Dune, Herbert demonstrates that while destruction is easy, preserving a complex system without flexibility is impossible.

Dune portrays politics as a slow, deliberate chess match—where the greatest moves are delayed, influence is amassed patiently, and the most powerful piece is not the one that strikes but the one unseen.

Religion as Algorithm

> *"When religion and politics travel in the same cart, the riders believe nothing can stand in their way. Their movements become headlong—faster and faster and faster. They put aside all thoughts of obstacles and forget that a precipice does not show itself to the man in a blind rush until it's too late."* — Frank Herbert, Dune

Herbert does not separate religion from politics—he reveals that within vast systems of governance, the two become nearly inseparable. In the universe of Dune, faith is not mere belief; it is an instrument powerful enough to unite civilizations, mobilize armies, and sanctify tyranny. Yet the more potent the instrument, the more perilous it becomes in the hands of the inept or self-serving.

A striking example is the Missionaria Protectiva—the Bene Gesserit program for seeding myths across the known universe. They plant religious prophecies generations ahead of actual events or figures, so that their agents—like Lady Jessica—can one day wield those beliefs for influence and control. This is not mysticism—it is engineered belief.

Paul Atreides becomes Muad'Dib precisely because he enters a carefully constructed religious framework. His arrival among the Fremen aligns exactly with their ancient legends—legends deliberately implanted by the Bene Gesserit. Thus, Paul uses religion to unite the Fremen, only to find himself trapped within the very prophecy he fulfills. He foresees the Jihad, dreads it, yet cannot stop it—for he has already become its symbol.

Herbert underscores a fundamental principle: in Dune, religion functions as a self-fulfilling prophecy. People first believe in something foretold—such as the coming of a Chosen One—and then act in ways that make that belief manifest. Their behavior begins to conform to expectation until, at last, the prophecy is fulfilled—not because it was inherently true, but because belief shaped action, and action shaped reality. So it was with Paul: the Fremen believed he was their messiah and followed him. In turn, he was compelled to lead them—down a path he never wished to take.

The circle closes: belief begets action, and action reinforces belief. In such a system, individual will is eroded—only the role imposed by collective faith remains.

If religion in Dune is a mechanism, then prophecy is its driving engine. The vision of the future becomes not a gift, but a philosophical trap. Paul, blessed—or cursed—with prescience, forfeits his freedom. He sees where the path leads but cannot divert it. His power gives rise to a war he never chose yet cannot prevent.

Herbert reveals absolute knowledge of the future renders free will illusory. For when one knows the outcome of every action, true choice dissolves.

One becomes not a sovereign actor but a performer—repeating lines in a play already written. Prescience narrows possibility to a single, unyielding trajectory. Will becomes obedience to inevitability, not an act of volition.

Leto II perceives this trap—and turns it into a weapon. His Golden Path is a calculated ordeal: a tunnel through which humanity must pass to one day reclaim the freedom to choose. He willingly becomes a monster—forsaking his own humanity—to grant future generations the chance to break free from the tyranny of prophecy.

Who, then, is the true victim: those who believe, or the one in whom belief is placed? In this, Dune redefines the archetype of the prophet—not as a blessed herald but as a tragic figure, condemned to see everything, and choose nothing. It is a haunting meditation on the cost of knowledge, the burden of faith, and the elusive nature of freedom.

Evolution—but at What Cost?

> «A process cannot be understood by stopping it. Understanding must move with the flow of the process, must join it and flow with it.» — Frank Herbert, Dune

Within the universe of Dune, evolution manifests not merely biologically but also culturally, technologically, and socially. Humankind endured the Butlerian Jihad, casting aside thinking machines and staking its future upon the development of humanity itself. Yet what is the price of this choice? Who are we, having replaced computers with Mentats, medicine with the manipulations of the Bene Tleilaxu, and instinct with Other Memory?

Herbert presents a spectrum of post-human paths—each a distinct evolutionary fork in the destiny of mankind:

- *Mentats* — logic pushed to its furthest extreme, stripped of impulse. Their minds outpace even machines, but the cost is steep: souls rendered pale and colorless.

- *The Bene Gesserit* — the path of mastery over body and spirit.

Their objective: sculpting a controlled future through selective breeding, relentless training, and precise behavioral conditioning. They refine the human being from within, not from without —as a jeweler transforms a concept into a gem. Their path is not born of love but necessity.

✦ *The Bene Tleilaxu* — masters of biological engineering and amoral adaptability. Gholas, Face Dancers, axlotl tanks—they represent an extreme: a humanity that relinquishes morality in pursuit of dominion over life itself. It is a path that erodes the line between what is natural and what is designed.

✦ *Leto II* — the apotheosis of transformation. He becomes a hybrid of human and sandworm, the eternal God Emperor whose body defies time and whose mind spans millennia. In this being, the human is no longer recognizable—only the vessel of the Golden Path endures. Herbert compels us to ask: can one remain humane while becoming fundamentally other-than-human?

All these divergent paths of development point toward a single truth: evolution is always a bargain. To gain strength, mastery, or longevity, something must be surrendered: emotion, the body, freedom, morality. None of these paths leads to an ideal outcome, yet each forces the same question: how far are we willing to reshape ourselves for the sake of survival? Where does humanity end if it is endlessly refined?

It is precisely for this reason that Dune transcends science fiction and becomes a philosophy of humankind in transformation. Herbert offers no blueprint for post-humanity—he delivers a warning: do not lose the soul of the human, even as you learn to become more than human.

The Survival of the Species: Leto II's Golden Path

> « *You cannot understand history unless you understand its flow. I made that flow visible. I made it stable. I made it purposeful.* » — *Leto II, God Emperor of Dune*

What is required to ensure humanity's salvation? In the universe of Dune, this question is not answered by laws, reforms, or technologies. Frank Herbert's answer is radical: salvation can only be achieved through pain, constraint, and absolute power. Leto II's Golden Path is no utopia—it is the deliberate throttling of progress to ensure humanity's survival not merely for the next generation but for millennia to come.

Leto II knew: left to its own impulses, humanity would inevitably destroy itself—whether through war, centralized oppression, or the perils of prescience. To avert catastrophe, he became what all feared: tyrant, god, worm. His body—an immortal shell; his mind—a vast repository of Other Memory; his will—an unyielding force restraining civilization to the Path.

He did not merely rule—he suffocated. He forbade mass migrations, curbed technological growth, and dismantled concentrations of power. All for a singular purpose: to render humanity scattered, adaptive, and immune to prediction. Only then could it be free from future tyranny and fate itself.

The Golden Path is a strategy for survival at the species level, not the individual. Herbert posits: individual liberty may be sacrificed if the objective is to preserve the possibility of choice for generations yet unborn. It is a brutal, yet profoundly farsighted logic.

The tragedy of Leto II lies in his renunciation of humanity to preserve humankind. He became monstrous so that humanity would no longer require monsters. This is Herbert's paradox: true virtue may wear the mask of horror when survival itself is the objective.

The Golden Path is not an endorsement of tyranny—it is a warning. Herbert does not say that oppression is righteous. He reveals that sometimes one must temporarily let it go to preserve freedom.

> A Question for Reflection: Am I prepared to follow a path, knowing its culmination will be witnessed only by others?

Leadership and Power: Heroism and Tyranny

Dune offers no hymn to great rulers; it presents an anatomy of power. Herbert does not romanticize leaders. He reveals how even the noblest intentions, ensnared within the structures of authority, may curdle into tyranny.

In this universe, power is no reward for virtue but a crushing burden, capable of irrevocably altering those who bear it.

Paul Atreides begins as a hero. He is just, intelligent, resolute. But upon attaining power—particularly power magnified by myth and prophecy—he loses control over the consequences unleashed. Thus, Herbert demonstrates that heroism devoid of critical reflection is itself a path to catastrophe.

Leto II learns from his father's errors. He does not struggle against the consequences of power—he seizes control of them. His tyranny is deliberate: he knows he will be reviled yet accepts this for the sake of his purpose. His reign is devoid of idealism—driven solely by calculation. And yet this does not make him 'evil.' He understands that to rule is not to express the will of the people, but to bear responsibility for their future.

Herein lies the essence of Herbert's approach: he dismantles the archetype of the noble king. No leader in Dune emerges as a savior. All are figures within a system where power inevitably distorts, and ideology serves merely as a mask. Herbert seems to caution: the danger is not the evil leader—the true danger lies with the one deemed virtuous without question.

True leadership, in Herbert's view, is not charisma and conquest. It resides in doubt, self-mastery, and the readiness for sacrifice. Power is not a pinnacle but an ordeal. And it is an ordeal through which few retain their essential humanity.

The entire philosophy of Dune—from political intrigues to the Golden Path—repeatedly returns us to this question: what is the price of power, and can one, in reshaping the world, preserve oneself? Herbert's answer offers little comfort, yet it is honest: only those who harbor doubt and strive not for personal gain but for the future, have a chance of not dissolving into the mechanism. For the rest, there remains only the playing out of a predetermined role—even if the audience applauds.

Dune offers no solace. It demands contemplation. All its themes—power, faith, choice, evolution—are interwoven into a single, pulsating organism where no absolute truths endure—only consequences. This part of the book has revealed: heroes are not always just, prophets are not always free, and salvation may arrive in monstrous guise.

PART IV: THE DUNE PHENOMENON: LEGACY AND YOUR JOURNEY

✧ ◆ ✧

This Part first explores that external legacy, the enduring life of the saga in the wider world. Then, turning the lens finally inward, it invites you to embark upon your own journey of reflection, continuing the dialogue after the book is closed.

Chapter 19: Life Beyond the Book

> « *The mystery of life isn't a problem to solve, but a reality to experience.* » — Frank Herbert

All that we have discussed so far—the characters, the themes, the ideas—forms the spine of Dune. Yet there is another life to it, one that begins after the final page is turned: discussions, debates, reinterpretations, the birth of new meanings. Dune has long since transcended the bounds of a single novel; it has become a cultural phenomenon, where canon, fandom, and the personal experience of every reader are interwoven.

What is considered canon?

The core canon of the Dune saga consists of Frank Herbert's six original novels, from Dune to Chapterhouse: Dune. These works embody the primary arc envisioned by the author—political, philosophical, ecological. Everything that came afterward—prequels, sequels, and the novels by Brian Herbert and Kevin J. Anderson—remains a subject of debate. For some, they represent a welcome expansion of the universe; for others, a form of fan fiction. Respecting differing views is an essential part of being in the fandom.

What is the Dune Fandom?

The Dune fandom is a remarkable space. Individuals are drawn to it for diverse reasons: some seek heroism; others philosophy, still others are captivated by the sands of Arrakis. It encompasses books, films, games, cosplay, translations, essays, memes, and endless debates about who was right: Paul or Leto. Here, there exists no single correct viewpoint—just as in Dune itself.

Why is Debate Good?

Because Dune is a living work. If you debate, disagree, pose questions—it signifies the work is alive within you. The very essence of the novels resides in this multiplicity of perspectives. Herbert offers no messiah demanding unquestioning belief. There are only ideas demanding interpretation and reflection.

Dune on Screen

The visual grandeur and conceptual depth of Dune have always beckoned filmmakers, yet translating its intricacies to the screen has proven a formidable challenge:

- *Jodorowsky's Dream (1970s)*: Alejandro Jodorowsky's unmade project entered history as 'the greatest film never made'. His radical, psychedelic vision, involving artists H.R. Giger and Moebius, left behind a now-legendary art book and profoundly influenced the aesthetics of science fiction for decades thereafter.

- *Lynch's Vision (1984)*: David Lynch's initial screen adaptation offered a surreal and baroque visual interpretation. Despite narrative compromises stemming from studio interference, its unique style, pervading atmosphere, and bold imagery ultimately secured the film enduring cult status.

- *Television Fidelity (2000, 2003)*: The Sci-Fi Channel miniseries (Frank Herbert's Dune and Frank Herbert's Children of Dune) proved that the television format could accommodate a more detailed adaptation, truer to the text, of the intricate source material. They garnered a warm reception from fans and were honored with Emmy Awards.

- *Villeneuve's Modern Epic (2021, 2024)*: Denis Villeneuve embraced the ambitious task on an unprecedented scale, dividing the first novel into two films. His approach—blending monumentality, grounded realism, and profound respect for the novel's spirit—earned rapturous reviews from critics and audiences alike, garnered numerous accolades (including six Academy Awards for Part One), and ignited a new wave of global interest in the saga. A planned third installment based on Dune Messiah promises to conclude his cinematic vision of the tragedy of Paul Atreides.

The Legacy and Influence of Dune

Dune is more than a series of books; it is a cultural phenomenon whose influence echoes across generations. Recognized as one of the greatest works of science fiction, the saga has sold tens of millions of copies and been translated into numerous languages. Its impact reaches far beyond literature:

- *A Pioneer of Ecology in Science Fiction*: Frank Herbert introduced themes of planetary ecology, terraforming, and the struggle over resources long before they entered mainstream discourse.

- *Inspiration for Generations*: The ideas, imagery, and terminology of Dune—the spice, the Fremen, the sandworms, the Mentats, the Bene Gesserit—have profoundly shaped the science fiction landscape, influencing giants such as Star Wars.

- *Philosophy and Culture*: The phrase 'Fear is the mind-killer' has become a lasting maxim. The saga continues to fuel debates on politics, religion, technology, and the nature of human potential.

- *Beyond the Books*: The universe of Dune spawned acclaimed tabletop and video games—the legendary Dune II laid the foundation for the real-time strategy genre.

The intricate layering of the world-building, founded upon Frank Herbert's immense research, coupled with the profundity of the questions it poses, ensure Dune's continuing, vital relevance.

For Whom is Dune?

Why is it worth reading (or rereading) this saga today? The world of Dune is complex. It grants no easy entry. Here resides no simple division between good and evil, no swift answers. Yet this is precisely why it continues to trouble the mind decades on. Dune is a book that grows with the reader. And the deeper one ventures into it, the more it yields in return..

For whom will it resonate?

For those who appreciate philosophical science fiction, wherein action is inseparable from underlying ideas. If you seek books that compel reflection — Dune is precisely such a work.

For those who relish intricate worlds. Ecology, politics, religion, language, history — all are interconnected. This is not merely backdrop but woven into the fabric of the narrative.

For those weary of simplistic heroes. Paul, Leto II, Jessica — these are not idealized figures but complex characters, imbued with contradictions, frailties, and capacity for growth.

For those who seek to read between the lines. In scenes where Paul foresees the repercussions of the Jihad, Herbert refrains from direct moral judgment. He presents the dilemma — offering no unambiguous resolution. Such is the operation of his philosophy: the reader is compelled to render judgment themselves.

Why Read Dune Again—and Again

Because Dune changes with the reader. In youth, it may read as the tale of a hero. In maturity, it becomes a parable of power and the cost of knowledge. With every rereading, one perceives details that previously eluded notice.

Why Now?

Because today, perhaps more than ever, the themes Herbert explores resonate with acute relevance: the manipulation of mass consciousness; ecology as a question of survival; the perils of charisma; the power of information. Dune does not merely speak of the future—it speaks to the present, veiled in the language of metaphor.

If you have yet to read Dune—begin. If you have read it—return to its sands. Within this sandstorm of ideas, you may find not answers, but a reflection of the self.

Your Journey

You are not an observer. You are a participant. Your interpretation, your moments of incomprehension, your elation or rejection—these, too, are part of the Dune phenomenon. None can read it for you. But if you have walked this path—from the first sands of Arrakis to the final thoughts of Leto II—then you are already inside.

And perhaps, this journey has only just begun.

Chapter 20: Dune as a Guide to Reality

Thus far, this guide has traced a path of analysis, seeking to systematize the intricate universe of Dune. The tone now deliberately shifts as we enter these final two chapters. We move from the question 'What is Dune?' toward the question 'What might Dune mean for us?'. Herein lies an attempt to contemplate certain concepts (Mentats, Fremen, Bene Gesserit) not merely as elements within Herbert's world, but as metaphors or models that might provoke reflection upon our own lives, our ways of thinking, and our capacity for adaptation. This is not a set of instructions but rather an invitation to perceive potential parallels.

Mentats: The Discipline of Thought

A Mentat is no prophet. It is a human being who thinks systemically, dispassionately, relying upon data rather than judgments.

What we might take from them:

✦ *Before reacting, ask*: What motive underlies this action?

✦ *Develop the habit of gathering data* — not opinions. Seek primary sources, not secondhand retellings.

✦ *Think in scenarios*: if X, then Y. Not one step ahead, but three.

✦ *Analyze not only the actions of others* — but also your own.

The Mentat is no mythical hero but the outcome of systematic thought. It represents a discipline of mind founded upon data, not upon emotional reaction.

> A Question for Reflection: In which spheres do I most often rely upon impulse, rather than upon analysis?

The Fremen: Adaptation as Strategy

The Fremen did not fight the desert. They befriended it. Where others chose struggle, they chose integration. Where others succumbed to fear, they chose strategy. This is the essence of resilience.

What we might take from them:

✦ *Minimalism* — not as fashion but a form of independence.

✦ *The strength of the collective*: a Fremen is not a lone hero but part of a tribe.

✦ *An enemy need not always be destroyed* — it can be ridden. They achieved this with the sandworms.

✦ *Adapt to the environment* — understanding its rhythms, not by trying to conquer it.

In the twenty-first century, we once again live amid instability. Fremen logic is not romanticism—it is a survival manual: less, deeper, together.

> A Question for Reflection: What in my life now demands not struggle, but acceptance and adaptation?

Bene Gesserit: Mastery of Context

The Sisters do not strike. They sow. Their power lies not in armies but in how a person thinks—sometimes a generation after encountering them.

What we might take from them:

- Language is power. Not only what is said, but how it is said shapes perception.

- We are the result of implanted narratives. Who planted in us ideas about success, happiness, and what we should strive for?

- The Bene Gesserit do not argue. They shape the ground upon which arguments are lost before they begin.

- Manipulation is not inherently evil. It depends upon the purpose it serves.

In an age of information floods, disinformation, and algorithmic influence, we do not need more data—we need the ability to perceive the structures beneath it. The Bene Gesserit embodied that vision.

> A Question for Reflection: What stories live within me that were planted there by others?

Each of these perspectives is not a solution but an invitation. An invitation to experiment. To observe. To comprehend yourself more deeply—through their lens.

Chapter 21: 10 Grains of Sand That Shift the Inner Dunes

« *To endure oneself may be the hardest task in the universe.* » — *Frank Herbert*

This collection of questions picks up the thread begun in the previous chapter—a journey from Herbert's world into your own inner landscape. It demands no specialized knowledge, only honesty. It offers no 'correct' answers, only the opportunity to truly hear oneself.

After each question, pause. An immediate answer is not required. Yet should one arise—record it.

1. What is fear—to me?

Herbert wrote: "Fear is the mind-killer." How do I typically react to fear—do I flee, fight, or pretend it does not exist?

> Reflect. If desired—record a few lines.

2. Where does faith end—and blindness begin?

How can one distinguish inspiration from manipulation? Who or what forms my convictions?

3. When do I truly make a choice, and when do I merely follow?

Paul Atreides became a symbol—and lost his freedom. Where in my own life might I risk confusing my path with a predetermined role?

4. What do I consider strength?

Silence, control, endurance, compassion? How do I relate to power—my own and that of others?

5. How open am I to perspectives different from my own?

Dune teaches that truth is always multi-layered. When did I last truly change my mind?

6. Do I believe in 'progress'—and what do I term 'development'?

Leto II placed humanity in stasis for the sake of its future. What matters more to me—movement or preservation?

7. Where lies my inner boundary of the acceptable?

The Tleilaxu effaced theirs for the sake of experiment. And myself? What, for me, is taboo, and what allows for flexibility?

8. What do I wish to leave behind?

The heroes of Dune rarely chose personal immortality—but their deeds endured. What will remain of me?

9. With whom would I stand upon Arrakis?

Fremen, Bene Gesserit, Mentat, researcher, observer? Why?

10. What, if anything, has changed within me after reading Dune?

Be it small or great. What matters is simply this—was there movement?

What Your Answers May Reveal

Your notes are not merely words but reflections of your inner landscape—a private map of your consciousness. When revisiting your responses, notice the following:

✦ Which themes resonated most strongly? Perhaps therein lie your true values, hidden fears, and areas for growth.

✦ Were some questions particularly difficult to confront? Difficulty or resistance may point toward topics that deserve deeper exploration.

✦ Have your answers evolved over time? Returning to your notes weeks or even years later can reveal shifts in your worldview and emotional state.

The answers themselves are merely a starting point. They do not define you; they illuminate your potential paths forward.

FINAL STEPS ON ARRAKIS

✧ ◆ ✧

If you have reached these lines, you have traveled a long and arduous road. From the first sands of Arrakis to the distant boundaries of the Golden Path; from the intrigues of the Landsraad to the profound depths of prescient philosophy. And if even one thought has lingered within you—if even once you paused in reflection—then none of this journey has been in vain.

Dune is more than mere science fiction

It is a mirror. A test of awareness—toward the world, toward others, toward oneself. It speaks not of a distant future, but of what is eternally near: fear, power, faith, choice, love. Each return to these pages is not merely an act of reading—it is a dialogue, one held not only with Herbert but with yourself.

I wrote this book as a fellow traveler, not an expert. As a reader for whom Dune once changed something essential. If it has helped you, too, then we are no longer alone in this desert. And that changes much.

May your reflections continue far beyond these pages.

Until we meet again—on other paths.

P.S. If this book helped you see Dune more clearly, I would be truly grateful for a brief review.

Your words may help other seekers find their way through the sands—and remind the author that the work still speaks.

Thank you for being here.

Printed in Dunstable, United Kingdom